Monster Doughnuts
BEASTLY BREAKOUT!

Books by Gianna Pollero, illustrated by Sarah Horne

Monster Doughnuts
Monster Doughnuts 2: Cyclops on a Mission
Monster Doughnuts 3: Beastly Breakout!

GIANNA POLLERO

illustrated by

Sarah Horne

Piccadilly
PRESS

First published in Great Britain in 2022 by
PICCADILLY PRESS
4th Floor, Victoria House, Bloomsbury Square, London WC1B 4DA
Owned by Bonnier Books
Sveavägen 56, Stockholm, Sweden
www.piccadillypress.co.uk

A CIP catalogue record for this book is available from the British Library.

ISBN: 978-1-80078-085-9
Also available in ebook and audio

1

Designed by Suzanne Cooper
Printed and bound in Great Britain by Clays Ltd, Elcograf S.p.A.

Piccadilly Press is an imprint of Bonnier Books UK
www.bonnierbooks.co.uk

For Maria, my best friend, without whom I would be useless (and life would be nowhere near as much fun).
And for her daughter, Amelie.

CHAPTER ONE

Where is Mr Harris?

Grace felt the stepladder wobble slightly as she reached the top. She passed the shiny red cherry to Kenny, her faithful little Key Catcher, who took it in his wiry hands and immediately leapt off her shoulder. He glided through the air smoothly, popping the cherry on the top of an enormous profiterole mountain as he passed it. He landed neatly on the other side of the table and took a bow.

'Well done, Kenny!' said Grace. 'I would never have had a steady enough hand to get that all the way up there. It's the biggest profiterole mountain I've ever seen.'

'It needs to be,' said Grace's older sister Danni, wiping her hands on her yellow apron. 'It'll be feeding over two hundred people at a wedding. I never want to see a profiterole again!'

'I'm glad that Mr Harris isn't here,' said Grace. 'He wouldn't be able to resist the profiteroles. We'd be replacing them every three seconds.'

'Is he still not answering his video phone?' said Danni, frowning.

Grace shook her head. 'I haven't been able to get hold of him since he left the party yesterday. I'm starting to get a bit worried.'

'He's a massive, rude, people-eaty cyclops,' said Danni. 'I'm sure he's fine. Have you found out any more about where he's heading?'

'W-well, we know he's gone to look for his m-mum, Gertrudetta,' said Frank, peering out from behind the profiterole mountain.

'And we know he'd been trying to locate her for some time,' added Grace. 'I don't think they've spoken for ages so I guess he wants to put things right. As strange as that is for Mr Harris!'

'The Monster Scanner information says that G-Gertrudetta lives in some sort of s-secret cave in the F-Forest of Fiends, in Monster World. The journey there is likely to be d-dangerous,' Frank said.

Grace nodded. 'There are woods and bridges and ravines, and goodness knows what else, to get past on the way to the forest. And you know how easily distracted he is! He'll be hungry, or tired, or bored, and he'll do something stupid, I know it.'

'Well, at least he took some of his celebration cake with him,' said Danni. 'Hopefully that will mean he's not hungry for a while.'

Grace sighed. 'Yes, probably for about five minutes,' she said. 'I'm going to try phoning him again. Perhaps if I tell him about the profiteroles, he'll come back.'

Danni shook her head vigorously as Grace pressed the redial button on the video phone and waited.

Just as she was about to hang up, a large yellowish eye filled the screen.

'What do you want, Doughnut Lady?' Mr Harris barked.

'Finally!' said Grace. 'I've been trying to get hold of you for hours! You left at the very start of your party, Mr Harris. If you'd told us that you were going to find your mum, we'd have come with you.'

The cyclops's angry eye filled the small screen. 'Didn't take you long to snoop around and find out where I was going, did it?' he snapped.

'You didn't hide it very well!' Grace retorted. 'Now, come back. Let's do this properly.'

The cyclops snorted. 'Properly? You're a monster hunter. I'm hardly going to lead you to my own flesh and blood, am I?'

Frank squeezed his face next to Grace's on the video phone screen and piped up, 'You're a m-monster hunter too.' The ornate golden fork he carried everywhere for protection glinted at the corner of the screen.

Mr Harris shook his head in disgust. 'No, I'm not, Shrimp Boy. I'm a monster. The BEST monster! And also a recently promoted Secret Service Senior Field Officer. The BEST Secret Service Senior Field Officer! I multitask.' He grinned self-importantly.

'Exactly!' said Grace.

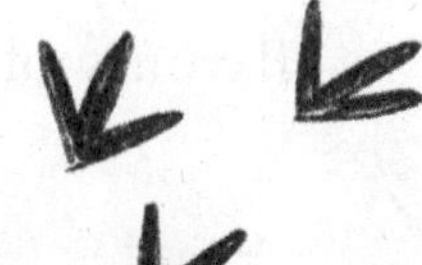

'So, what if you're needed here? You might be given another case today.'

'You can do it – I'm very busy,' said Mr Harris dismissively. Then his eye opened wider. 'What's that behind you? Is it a mountain of profiteroles?'

Grace swung round so the chocolatey choux buns were out of sight. 'Oh, that's nothing, it's fake, you know, just for display. So, what exactly are you doing at the moment?' She tried to peer behind the massive cyclops. 'And *where* are you?'

'I'm staying with an associate before I embark on my journey,' he replied. 'And now I must go. So stop phoning me and annoying me and –'

'Mr 'Arris! Come 'ere! I 'ave another amazing flavourrr for you to trrry!' came an Italian-accented voice from somewhere behind Mr Harris.

'You're with Marietto! You're eating ice cream!' cried Grace.

'Shhhh,' hissed the cyclops. 'Don't you dare ruin this for me. I've tried forty-four flavours of ice cream and I am not stopping now. He can't know that you're trying to track me down. He'll hand me over in a second! I've never known a Gelato Guzzler that's so well behaved and sensible. He's ridiculous – the most un-monstery monster in history. But he makes excellent ice cream so go away, Doughnut Lady. I'm about to try double chocolate coconut swirl with a hint of Earl Grey. I've been waiting for ages to try this one. And you, with your beaky nose and your snoopy little eyes and your meddling computer fingers, are not going to stop me.'

He hung up.

'He seems perfectly fine,' said Danni.

Frank nodded. 'Very n-normal.'

'He's a pain in the neck,' said Grace. 'But if he's eating ice cream, he's going nowhere for a while. And that means we have a bit more time to research the Forest of Fiends before we actually have to go down the rickety ladder to Monster World and find him ourselves.'

CHAPTER TWO

Emergency!

'So, what do we know?' asked Max, Frank's dad, leaning across a table at the back of the bakery to look at the information Grace and Frank had found.

'Well, there are a couple of routes to the Forest of Fiends and we've identified a couple of areas that are likely to have caves, so we think they're probably the best places to start,' replied Grace. Kenny was sitting on her shoulder, his wiry legs draped over her collar bone.

Grace's dad, Eamon cleared his throat. 'A lot of monsters live in the Forest of Fiends, and that alone makes it dangerous. We need a plan to –'

A shrill ring interrupted him.

He pulled his video phone out of his pocket.

'It's Colonel Hardy,' he said, referring to the Head of the Secret Service. 'Hello, Colonel, what a nice surprise to hear from you so soon after the last assignments.'

'There's no time for niceties, Mr Hunter,' said the immaculately dressed woman on the screen. 'We have an emergency.'

Grace, Kenny still on her shoulder, her mum Louisa, Danni, Max and Frank gathered around Eamon.

'There's been a major incident in Monster World,' the Colonel said briskly. 'Approximately two hours ago, forty-three monsters who were serving prison sentences in the imaginatively named Monster World Prison managed to escape. All but one remain at large. We have reason to believe that some of these monsters were Neville Harris's followers, with whom Neville Harris had intended to take over Human World. We must act fast.'

Eamon raised his eyebrows, speechless.

'Oh my goblins,' whispered Frank.

Colonel Hardy continued. 'You will be the Task Force on this case. I suggest that Mr Harris and three Hunters head directly to Monster World, while the remaining three Hunters stay here to intercept any monsters who make it through the gateways. We cannot let this situation get out of control, can we, *Mr Harris*?'

Grace felt her heart beat faster as Colonel Hardy's gaze moved over the faces on her screen.

'Where *is* Mr Harris?' she asked, frowning.

'Bathroom!' blurted Grace at the same time as Danni said, 'Napping!'

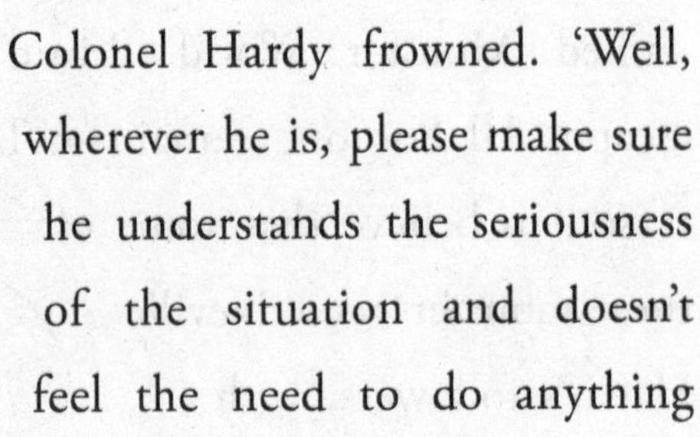

Colonel Hardy frowned. 'Well, wherever he is, please make sure he understands the seriousness of the situation and doesn't feel the need to do anything unbelievably, mind-numbingly stupid. I'll be calling in on you frequently. You must contact me straight away if you have any significant progress to report.'

'Colonel Hardy?' ventured Grace. 'May I ask a question?'

The Colonel nodded curtly.

'You said that all but one of the monsters are still at large,' said Grace. 'What type of monster has been recaptured? Can we get any information from it about what happened, or about what the escaped monsters plan to do?'

'Good question, Grace, but don't get excited,' the Colonel replied. 'The recaptured monster was an elderly goblin who fell asleep in the grass after he ran across the prison exercise field and wore himself out. One of the prison officers tripped over him and carried him back inside. He's being questioned now but, the last I heard, they're struggling to keep him awake. I don't think he's going to be your best lead.'

The screen went blank. The Hunter family remained quiet.

'A Monster Prison break?' said Eamon. 'Never in all my years of monster-hunting . . .'

'Well, that decides our plan for us. We need to find Mr Harris now,' said Max. 'Looking at the information Grace and Frank printed off, Monster World Prison is on the way to the Forest of Fiends. Whether he likes it or not, he's going to have to help. He's part of our team, and Colonel Hardy is already suspicious about where he is.

He can keep watch for prisoners while he's on his way to find his mum.'

Grace frowned. 'He won't be happy when we track him down.'

Max shrugged. 'He might end up being grateful if we warn him before he comes across any of the escapees. I dread to think which monsters might have escaped . . . and what they could be capable of.'

CHAPTER THREE

Wanted!

After several more failed attempts to get through to Mr Harris on his video phone, Grace sent him a text message. She knew he hated messages, because he found it hard to type a reply with his sausage-like fingers, but she didn't have a choice. She needed to speak to him.

Answer your phone! There's an emergency and I need to speak to you. G

His response came quickly. Sausagey fingers or not, he was clearly quite capable of answering texts and calls.

No thanks.

You don't know how serious this is! I'll call you now. G

I am unavailable.

You're texting! I'm calling NOW. Answer it please! G

Grace pressed the 'call' button. After well over a minute, the screen burst into life, magnifying Mr Harris's already large eye so much that it filled the screen.

'Oh! Move the phone back a bit – all I can see is your eye!' she said.

'That's all you need to see, Doughnut Lady. Now what's the problem? I've been gone a few hours and already you can't cope. It's ridiculous. You Hunters are a needy breed,' the cyclops said.

'If you can stop moaning for a minute, I'll tell you what's happened. It *is* an emergency!' said Grace.

'Prime Minister lost her left sock?' mumbled the cyclops, more of his wide face coming into view. 'Does the Colonel need me to find her sense of humour?'

'There's been a prison break in Monster World!' exclaimed Grace. 'Forty-three monsters have escaped and only one has been captured so far. We must get them all back into prison before they do anything terrible. And if you didn't know already, Monster Prison is on the way to the Forest of Fiends, so you're going to need to be careful.'

The video phone's screen stopped moving and the cyclops said nothing for a few seconds. He snorted. 'Careful! Me? I'm a machine, Doughnut Lady.' Then he asked, 'How long have the prisoners been outside the prison grounds?'

'A good couple of hours,' Grace replied.

'There's no point looking, then,' Mr Harris said briskly. 'They'll be long gone, the rascals. Never mind, I'll just carry on doing what I'm doing.' He hung up.

'Did he just cut you off?' asked Danni from behind the bakery's counter, where she was gathering the special cakes. The ones that were used to explode monsters.

Grace nodded, frowning.

'Don't worry,' said Frank. 'You were on long enough for me to trace the call. It's not very accurate, because he's in M-Monster World, but it doesn't look like he's gone very far. I think he's probably still at Marietto's eating ice cream.'

'Frank, you're a genius!' said Danni, emptying a tray of well-risen muffins into a yellow paper bag and handing it to Grace.

'There's no time to lose,' said Max. 'Grace and Frank, we'll go to Monster World. We need to take anything that could help us, without weighing ourselves down too much.'

Kenny the Key Catcher leapt up and down on Grace's shoulder, pointing at himself with his spindly fingers.

'You will definitely be a help, Kenny, and you're as light as a feather. Don't worry, you're coming with us,' said Max.

The Key Catcher punched the air.

'We should stay here,' Louisa said to Eamon and Danni. 'We can monitor the Monster Scanner and take care of any monsters that make it through the gateway.' As she spoke, Eamon's phone bleeped.

'That'll be a list of the escaped monsters coming through,' he said, glancing down at the screen then pulling a face.

'What's the matter?' asked Louisa.

'I'm hoping that these monsters aren't listed from the least scary at number one to the most scary at number forty-three,' he said.

'W-Why?' asked Frank. 'What's number one?'

Eamon turned the screen round for everyone to see.

WANTED

Monster Number 1: Johnny Big-Hands

Non-compliant Giant.

Serving 132 years for bone-crushing.

Name: Jonathan Robert Ernest Big-Hands (a.k.a. Johnny Big-Hands)

Type: Non-compliant Giant

Age: Approximately 37 years

Height: 2.81 m

Weight: 424 lb

Strengths: 3 detected – strength, height, hand size.

Weaknesses: 4 detected – clumsy, moany, always hungry, tires easily.

Likes: Jelly, sleeping, small domestic pets such as mice and rats, camping, dolls' houses, Monster Prison, silly jokes, bone-crushing.

Dislikes: Exercise, hard work, early starts, grapes.

Best form of destruction: A bulldozer full of baking powder, or a very large number of florentines.

Notes: Mahoosive.

SCORING:

Friendship: 50

Size: 100

Courage: 29

Kindness: 35

Intelligence: 22

Loyalty: 54

Violence: 87

Danger: 91

Type: Medium rare

Location: Recently escaped from Monster Prison. Likely to be in the Forest of Fiends region.

CHAPTER FOUR

One Down

Less than forty minutes later, half the Hunters and Kenny were striding through the Natural History Museum towards the T-Rex animatronic display. The rather unextraordinary gateway to Monster World sat just behind the backdrop to the roaring dinosaur, in the form of a trapdoor.

'Look!' Grace said as they hurried past a large glass cabinet full of ancient pieces of pottery.

A very unhuman-looking leg was poking out from behind it. Although it was mostly covered with a black and white trouser leg, a hairy, foot caught Grace's attention.

'Our first escapee!' cried Max, slowing down. 'If that grotty trotter doesn't belong to a Tripper Upper, then I need to give up monster-hunting here and now. But Tripper Uppers are hardly dangerous, so I wonder why it was in prison.'

'Got it, Dad!' said Frank, pressing the tiny screen strapped to his wrist. 'Monster number thirty-two: Randolph Stumble-Jones, Tripper Upper. Serving seven life sentences for tripping people up in dangerous locations.'

'Wow,' said Grace, shaking her head in disbelief. 'I thought they were almost completely harmless.'

'They usually are,' said Max. 'This one must have gone rogue. Grace, you do the honours – you'll be more accurate than me, I'm sure.' He gestured towards his missing arm – the result of a terrible injury he had suffered years before on a particularly dangerous monster hunt.

Grace crept towards the black and white leg, holding a pot of baking powder she had taken

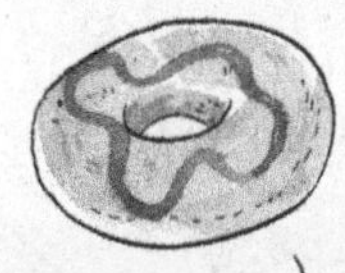

from her pocket. She edged to the corner of the cabinet and then, quick as a flash, whipped round and showered baking powder over the thin-lipped, narrow-eyed Tripper Upper, which was wearing a full Monster Prison jumpsuit.

It leapt forward to attack, both legs pushed out to their maximum length. But as it lurched towards Grace, there was a sharp *crack* and the monster disintegrated into a cloud of red dust, which smelled distinctly of pickles.

From another of Grace's pockets, Kenny held up his tiny hand so she could high-five him with her pinkie finger. Max phoned the incident through to Colonel Hardy's office and they continued towards the dinosaurs.

The dinosaur room wasn't especially busy, so they didn't have to wait long to sneak, unseen, behind the backdrop. Grace and Frank opened the trapdoor and the group hurried down the rickety ladder that would take them to Monster World. Several rungs of the ladder had changed since their last visit, so they had to watch where they trod. A cricket bat, a didgeridoo, a walking stick, a snowboard, several skis, a witch's broom, an ironing board and what looked like a dried mammoth's trunk made up the rungs.

'There's no troll guarding the bottom!' said Grace, peering down. 'Mr Harris must have eaten it.'

'No surprise there,' said Max, jumping off the bottom rung of the ladder. 'Right, we need to decide which route we're going to take to the Forest of Fiends. We need to take the one Mr Harris is likely to choose, so we can find him as quickly as possible. There were two routes that looked about the same distance when I checked the map earlier. One is far more dangerous than the other, though.'

'Is one even just a metre shorter?' asked Grace. 'Because that will be the one Mr Harris will take. He's incredibly lazy.'

'One is twenty-two metres shorter,' Frank replied.

'Well, that's the one we need to follow,' said Grace.

Frank sighed. 'Dad was right when he said that

one route was far more d-dangerous. I've looked at the M-Monster World map.'

Kenny, perched on Grace's shoulder, covered his face with his hands. He had clearly guessed what was coming next.

'It'll be the one he's chosen, without a doubt,' said Grace, pulling her video phone out of her pocket to call Mr Harris and warn him.

Frank nodded.

'That cyclops is a liability,' she muttered, and once again pressed 'dial'.

CHAPTER FIVE

Betsy

Mr Harris heard the video phone ring from inside the pocket of his tweed jacket. He sighed loudly and murmured, 'For goodness' sake, it's like they can't *breathe* without me being there.' He pulled out the phone and prodded the 'end call' button.

'Not now, Doughnut Lady,' he said. 'I'm busy. And you're a nuisance.'

He unfolded the map he had just bought from the Wart-n-Bones bookshop and studied it. He ran a meaty finger along the main road, through Monster World and up towards Red Rock Ravine, on the other side of which stood the Forest of Fiends.

'Two roads. This one . . . the MW1 monster-way and this one . . .' He read aloud from the notes on the map. 'The A13, known to some monster hikers as the Treacherous Track of Doom.' He laughed. 'Well, the A13 is clearly shorter. Why would I even consider taking the monster-way? Why put it on the map at all? Stupid map people! Easiest decision I've ever made. Now, I need a bicycle. I can't possibly walk all that way.'

He headed down the main road, which was bumpy and uneven. Dust billowed out of the gaps between the cobbles, and a peculiar, Brussels sprouty smell hung in the air. Monster chatter carried on the breeze and, somewhere nearby, a brass band was playing. Very badly.

Nosily, Mr Harris looked in the windows of the higgledy-piggledy shops he passed. They contained displays of clothes, shoes, DIY equipment, toys, soft furnishings, live snacks – everything a monster could need. As he neared the end of the buildings, where the road split in two, he spotted a sign. It said *Hot-to-Trot Transport*. Underneath, in smaller letters, it said: *For all your transport needs – we have bikes, scooters, pogo sticks and space hoppers! Or do you fancy something different? We stock donkeys fresh from Human World (straw hat not included in basic price)!*

Mr Harris's eye lit up and he picked up his pace.

'Donkeys,' he whispered. 'How grand.'

As he gripped the handle to the shop door, he felt a vibration against his huge belly then heard a familiar ring tone. His video phone had once again sprung to life. He snatched it out of his pocket and jabbed the 'answer' button.

'This had better be good, Doughnut Lady,' he snapped. 'I'm about to get me a donkey.'

An elegant face popped up onto the screen, dark hair pulled back into a pristine bun, shirt collar pressed into perfect points.

'Urgh!' cried the cyclops, taken by surprise. 'Captain Tardy! Mrs Lardy! Colonel Farty! HARDY! I meant Hardy!'

Colonel Hardy stared at him, unblinking, from the screen. 'Did you say something about a donkey, Mr Harris?'

He shook his head. 'No. I did not.'

'I'm sure you did,' she replied. 'I do hope you're taking this mission seriously.

If those escaped monsters are not found quickly, the fallout could be catastrophic.'

The cyclops nodded. 'Catas-TROPHIC!' he repeated, yelling the last part of the word to cover up a loud *hee-haw*.

Colonel Hardy narrowed her eyes. 'Are you on your own? Where are the Hunters?'

Mr Harris's own eye grew wider. His gaze darted from left to right, then he turned his head and checked over his shoulder, down the road. 'Oh, for goodness' sake,' he said. 'They must have fallen behind again. I seem to be the only one taking this mission seriously, Colonel Lady! They've probably been distracted by some nice rat-skin cushions or a delicious double maggot burger back at the shops. They're so unprofessional. Good job I'm here. Me, the diligent and expeditious *Senior Field Officer*.' He flashed her a smug grin.

Colonel Hardy grimaced. 'Yes, well, that's not quite how I would have put it,' she said firmly.

'I want regular updates, Mr Harris. I don't like to be kept waiting, especially on a mission as important as this one. I want you to phone me with a progress report in one hour. Goodbye.'

'*I want, I want, I want,*' he mimicked as he replaced the phone in his pocket and pushed open the door to Hot-to-Trot Transport. 'Well, Colonel Farty, before you get anything, *I* want a donkey.'

'You can't have a donkey,' said the mean-looking goblin sitting behind the counter, before Mr Harris had even closed the door behind him.

'Why not?' the cyclops whined.

'Because you'll flatten it. You're ginormous,' the goblin replied rudely.

'I'm broad, and I have dense bones!' Mr Harris shouted. 'Give me a donkey! That one!' He pointed to a little brown donkey wearing a straw hat. It was tethered to an old bicycle with a very small front wheel and a huge back wheel.

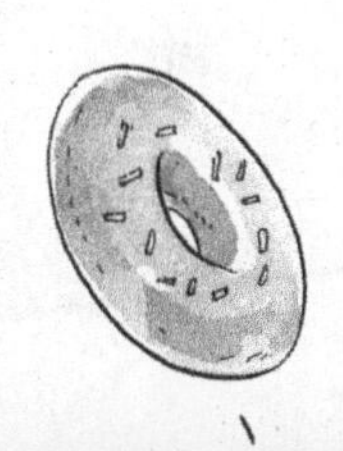
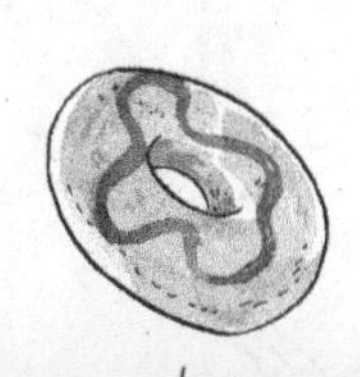

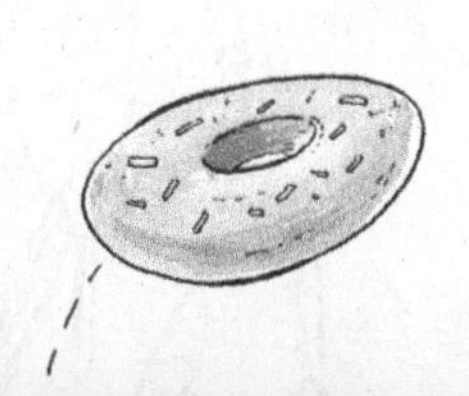

'No,' hissed the goblin. 'These donkeys are my bestsellers. I can't afford for one to be brought back probably as flat as a pancake, looking at you. And besides, Betsy comes with the bike. They're a package for couples.'

'I'll take both,' said Mr Harris firmly.

'Which will you be riding?' sneered the goblin.

'The ridiculous bicycle,' said Mr Harris slowly and menacingly.

'Then what do you want Betsy for?' said the goblin.

'I might get hungry. Doesn't look like that bike is going to go very fast, so pedalling will help me work up an appetite,' snapped Mr Harris. Then, seeing the goblin's expression, he blurted, 'Company! Betsy will keep me company and guide the way.'

'You're lying . . .' the goblin started.

Mr Harris sighed loudly. 'I can pay in human cake,' he said somewhat reluctantly. Goblins were greedy creatures and most had a very sweet tooth, so Mr Harris knew that the mention of cake would get his attention.

The shopkeeper's red eyes lit up. He glanced round the room, checking there were no other customers. 'Human cake?' he said, saliva glistening at the corners of his grey lips.

The cyclops nodded and opened his bag for life to flash the contents.

The goblin's gnarled hand shot out.

Mr Harris snapped his carrier bag shut and batted the goblin's hand away. 'Steady on, Nigel,' he said, reading the goblin's faded name badge. 'There's business to be done first. Now, can I have Betsy and her stupid bike, or not?'

Nigel nodded enthusiastically. 'Take all the donkeys if you want!' he gabbled, his beady gaze not moving from the bag.

Mr Harris plunged his hand inside and pulled out the smaller of the two cakes. He plopped it onto the counter and turned away immediately.

'Hardest thing I've ever had to do,' he said, heading towards Betsy and the oddly proportioned bike.

'Leave the straw hat on the floor, it's not included,' came a muffled cry from the goblin, whose mouth was already full of cake.

Mr Harris snorted. 'Absolutely not. You get my cake. I get your hat.' He took the straw boater from the donkey's head and placed it on top of his own hat. Then he hung the bag containing the remaining cake over the bicycle's handlebars and led his strange new purchases out of the shop.

CHAPTER SIX

Thief!

'He's still not answering!' said Grace, turning to Frank and Max.

Kenny shook his head in disappointment.

'You know he'll get himself into trouble. He'll fall down a hole or get attacked by a Shadow Stalker or . . . oh!' She stumbled and nearly lost her footing.

Max grabbed her rucksack and pulled her upright.

'Well done, Grace, you just found our next prisoner! This one looks like it won't be much of a challenge,' he said brightly, pointing at the

Sleep Stealer that was snoring loudly in the middle of the pavement.

'Oh! It's an interesting colour for a Sleep Stealer, isn't it? I thought they were usually grey,' said Grace, noticing the creature's dark orange, velvety fur. 'Why was it in prison, Frank? They usually just like waking people up. Annoying, but hardly a crime.'

'I'm checking the list,' said Frank, his eyes glued to the device on his wrist. 'Here it is, let's see . . . number twenty-four, Brandy McNap, Sleep Stealer. Serving four years for the theft of two oatmeal biscuits, a pair of wellington boots and a glass of milk.'

'Four years!' cried Grace. 'If that Sleep Stealer got four years, Mr Harris should be serving twenty for the number of cakes he's taken from the bakery without asking!'

Max laughed. 'It's Monster World, Grace. There's no logical reason for the punishments.'

'Dad, what do we do with the prisoners when

we've found them?' asked Frank, staring at the Sleep Stealer, which was contentedly dozing, a line of dribble hanging from one side of its mouth.

'If they pose no danger, we can just secure them and take them back to one of the designated drop-off points – we have a list from Colonel Hardy – or we can take them back to Monster World Prison if we're close enough. But if we come across one that's fighty and dangerous, we explode it. As quickly as possible,' Max replied. 'We'll drop this one off. I don't think it's likely to attack any time soon.'

Frank prodded the creature with his toe, then with his hand. When it remained fast asleep, Grace leaned down and shook it gently.

'Er, Brandy McNap, you need to come with us,' she said. 'Sorry.'

The creature didn't stir.

Kenny leapt down from Grace's shoulder and onto the creature's chest. He twanged one of its whiskers. Nothing.

'Shall I just p-pick it up?' asked Frank. 'It doesn't look heavy. We can take it in turns to carry it, Grace.'

Grace shrugged.

Frank squatted next to the creature, which was about the size of a rabbit, and gently lifted it up. He tried to prop it against his shoulder but it flopped back into his arms, sound asleep.

Grace giggled. 'Your baby looks weird.'

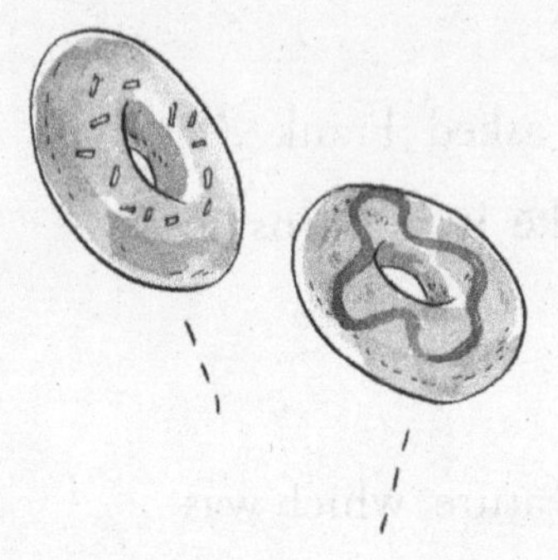

Frank chuckled. 'Not in M-Monster World it doesn't! And for a nice change, this one doesn't smell too bad.' He sniffed. 'A bit like lavender, actually.'

'Right, let's call Colonel Hardy,' Max said. 'We can tell her we've caught the least threatening monster that ever lived.'

Grace passed him the video phone.

Colonel Hardy answered after one ring. 'Mr Hunter,' she said briskly.

'Hello, Colonel,' said Max. 'I'm just calling with a progress report. We've secured our first escapee in Monster World. It's not the most exciting one, but it's detained nonetheless. Number twenty-four, Brandy McNap, Sleep Stealer.'

Colonel Hardy frowned and glanced over Max's shoulder on the screen. 'Is Frank holding it like a baby?' she asked.

'It's very sleepy,' Grace chimed in. 'It only

stole a couple of biscuits, some milk and a pair of wellies, so we think it's pretty tame.'

'Very well. Let's hope you find a more murderous one next,' said Colonel Hardy, ending the call.

Max handed the video phone back to Grace and the group continued to make their way along the main road through Monster World. Strange smells and noises escaped from the higgledy-piggledy buildings that lined the street.

'Is that a trumpet I can hear?' asked Max, frowning and looking round for the source of the metallic whine.

They passed several monsters, most of which didn't give them a second glance. A couple of Gossip Givers whispered to one another excitedly as a Prank Cranker crept up behind them with a water balloon.

'I'm going to phone Mr Harris again,' said Grace, pressing the dial button on her video phone and holding it up in front of her.

This time, the cyclops's face appeared on the screen, chin first.

'What now, Doughnut Lady? I'm busy,' he said.

'Where are you?' asked Grace. 'And why am I looking at your chin?'

The cyclops rolled his eye. 'You're in my basket.'

'Basket?' questioned Grace.

'Yes!' the cyclops snapped. 'The basket on the bike I have acquired.'

Grace raised her eyebrows. 'Oh, okay.' She turned the phone away from her for a moment and mouthed to Frank and Max, 'He's left Marietto's!' Quickly she turned the screen towards her again. 'You don't seem to be going very fast if you're on a bike. And can I hear clip-clopping? Is there a horse near you? Do they have horses in Monster World?'

'You're going off topic, Doughnut Lady,' Mr Harris barked. 'What do you want?'

'We're here in Monster World, and I want you to come and find us,' said Grace. 'We need to do this together, as a team. You help us find the prisoners, we help you find your mum.'

'Oh good. You're here too,' said the cyclops with no enthusiasm whatsoever. 'Now, listen, you have your mission – and I have my own, more exciting, better mission. I know you will fail yours miserably without me –'

Grace interrupted. 'No, we won't! And it's OUR mission. We all need to work together. Plus, I was thinking, Mr Harris, what if you do a brilliant job again and you get another promotion?'

The cyclops paused, staring intently at her. 'Another promotion? What do you mean?'

'I mean, if you help to get all the prisoners back to Monster World Prison, there's a chance you could get another promotion. Surely you'd like that?' she said, playing to the cyclops's huge sense of self-importance.

'Do the jobs go higher than Senior Field Officer? I thought I was the highest already?' Mr Harris said.

'Head of Operations,' Max called.

The cyclops's eyebrow arched in interest. 'Head of Operations,' he repeated slowly.

All was quiet, until there was a screech behind him. '*Hee-haw*!'

'Hush, Betsy!' he bellowed. 'I'm thinking.'

'Betsy?' asked Grace. 'Who on earth is Betsy?'

As she tilted the video phone so Frank could get a look at whatever Betsy was, a spindly hand, with sharp claws on its fingers, came out of nowhere and snatched it. The owner of the hand sprinted away at speed, the legs of its black and white Monster World Prison jumpsuit flapping wildly in the breeze.

CHAPTER SEVEN

Cyclops in Charge

Mr Harris glared at the screen as Grace's video phone jerked up and down and hurtled this way and that.

'What *are* you doing, Doughnut Lady? You're making me feel sick. Keep still!' he shouted. 'Tell me more about this promotion.'

He heard a whoop of triumph and a throaty giggle. In the background, he heard someone shout, 'NO! Come back here now!'

'This is absolute chaos,' he mumbled. 'All I can see is the ground. Hold it up, for goodness' sake. Oh! What on earth are you doing? You've lost your mind!' He watched as the phone screen filled with pointy teeth and a leathery tongue. Then it became rather dark.

'That girl is feral,' he said, shaking his head. 'One minute she's all about teamwork and rules, the next she's swallowed her video phone in protest at my independence.'

The second he placed his video phone back inside the pocket of his tweed jacket, it rang again.

He breathed heavily through his nose. 'You've got to be joking. How has she got it back so quickly?'

He stopped pedalling and jabbed the 'answer' button. 'That was, quite frankly, disgusting. Now, tell me more about the promotion and then I will decide if I can be bothered to help you on your pointless prisoner project.'

The line remained silent. The cyclops glared at the screen and recoiled in shock. Once again,

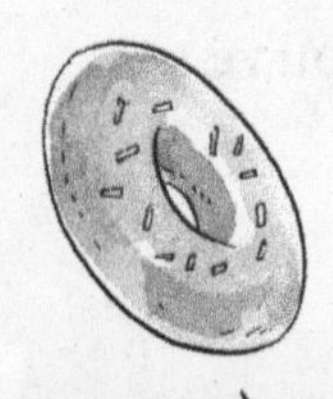
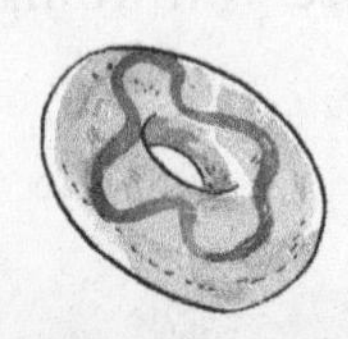

Colonel Hardy looked up at him, unblinking.

'I have many questions for you, Mr Harris,' she said quietly but very firmly. 'But, for now, we will start with one, on which I should have pressed you more when we last spoke. I'm concerned that you don't seem to be with the Hunters. So, where are you?'

The cyclops looked around frantically. 'Well, I'm here,' he said, gesturing to a large, square, grey building behind him.

Colonel Hardy seemed unamused. 'And where is *here*, Mr Harris?' she said. Then she narrowed her eyes. 'Hold on, is that the Monster World Authorities Headquarters?'

Mr Harris scanned a towering sign just behind him. He sniggered at his unbelievable good luck. 'Yes. Yes, it is. I came here to check in, as Senior Field Officer, to . . . er . . . reassure the . . . er . . . authorities that I will personally oversee the very important operation to catch all those stupid prisoners,' he said, making it up as he went along.

'Good old-fashioned customer service!'

'Is it indeed?' said Colonel Hardy, looking suspicious.

The cyclops nodded. 'I think, since I'm in charge of this mission, it's important that they know how excellent I am at my job. You never know, I might even get a promotion!' He laughed loudly and flashed Colonel Hardy his most charming grin.

'I see,' said Colonel Hardy. 'I wasn't aware that I had put you in charge. So if that's the case, tell me, where is your team?'

Mr Harris's eye widened. 'Well, they, er, they're . . . not here right now . . .'

'Explain,' the Colonel said.

'I sent them to gather information and catch more prisoners while I do the important things,' Mr Harris improvised.

'Of course you did,' replied Colonel Hardy flatly. 'I'm going to take this opportunity to remind you, Mr Harris, that the most important thing about this mission is to catch the escaped prisoners as quickly as possible.'

'Easy-peasy, lemon squeezy,' said the cyclops.

Colonel Hardy took a deep breath and closed her eyes for a few seconds. 'Let's hope so,' she said briskly. 'And, Mr Harris, I will just say one other thing. I don't know what you're up to, or why there is a donkey behind you, but please don't forget that you can get *demoted* just as easily as you can get *promoted* when you don't do your job properly, or take missions seriously. Perhaps you could give that some thought while you're practising your outstanding customer service with the Monster World Authorities.'

When the screen went blank, Mr Harris

smiled smugly at Betsy. 'Pulled that off. I am unbelievably quick-witted and clever. But I don't need her on my case again today.' He pressed the button on the top of the video phone and turned it off. 'Much better,' he said. Then he turned to the flat, grey Monster World Authorities Headquarters, which had a huge, sparkling

golden crown perched wonkily on top of the sign on the roof. 'Now, while I'm here, I might as well pop in and let them know they have the top Senior Field Officer dealing with their careless prison break!'

He tethered Betsy and the odd-looking bike to some spiky metal railings and strode towards the building. He was almost at the entrance when he turned, shuffled back and snatched the blue bag for life from the handlebars of the bike.

'I'm not leaving my cake unattended,' he murmured.

CHAPTER EIGHT

Gotcha!

'Oh no you don't!' said Grace, sprinting after the gangly monster that had stolen her video phone. It was about the same height as Grace, with long, lithe limbs. As well as its standard prison jumpsuit, it wore futuristic square glasses with mirrored lenses and a shiny silver baseball cap.

Grace was certain it was a Tech Taker – a relatively common, but rarely seen, monster. She remembered reading about them on the Monster Scanner just a few days before – she knew they couldn't resist a nice, shiny electronic device and would steal any they could get their hands on.

Unfortunately, they didn't steal them to play with them or to sell them. Generally, they ate them. Tech Takers' diets consisted of mobile phones, dismantled laptops and tortilla chips.

Grace was getting closer to the monster when it veered sharply to the left and disappeared. When she turned the same corner, she found a dead end. And no monsters.

A big black wheelie bin sat next to a door with a *Closed* sign in the window and a faded sign advertising an escape room. It was eerily quiet. Grace stood still and listened. The Tech Taker had to be somewhere close by. She gently pushed the door. It didn't give, so she thought it was unlikely that the monster had escaped into the escape room. Kenny bounced on her shoulder, pointing to the lock on the door.

'Not yet, Kenny,' she whispered.

As Frank and Max jogged round the corner, she held her finger to her lips.

She could hear a scuffling, scratching sound. Kenny pointed to the wheelie bin. Grace tiptoed over, Frank and Max behind her. Kenny held his spindly fingers up and counted down from three. As soon as Kenny got to one, they flung open the lid of the bin.

'Oh my g-goblins!' cried Frank.

Inside was not just one Tech Taker, but a variety of monsters; Grace counted six, sandwiched together like sardines in a tin. Five of them had their gnarly fingers to their lips and were glaring at the Tech Taker, who was scratching his armpit enthusiastically.

'Close the lid!' yelled Max.

Just as a couple of the monsters looked ready to leap out, they banged the lid shut.

'It'll be too difficult to keep control of them all at once,' he said. 'So let's keep them in the bin and wheel them back to prison. Frank, sit on the lid! Kenny, can you help keep it shut?'

The little Key Catcher leapt from Grace's shoulder onto the bin lid and flexed his tiny arms until two round biceps popped up. Then he dived onto his front and lay flat, hooking his forearms and hands over the rim. They were so wiry that they could mould to the shape perfectly. He gave a quick thumbs-up then immediately resumed his position. Grace and Max helped Frank onto the top of the bin. Brandy McNap the Sleep Stealer still snored peacefully in his arms. A series of thuds, shoves and hisses came from inside the bin, but the lid held still.

'Right, I'll help you push,' Grace said to Max. 'I can't believe there were so many in there. I wonder who we've caught from the wanted list.'

'We won't be able to check until we get to the prison. There's no way we can open that lid – they'll all run off in different directions and we'll be back to square one,' said Max.

Grace nodded. 'There was definitely a Pickpocket Pixie in there – nothing else has such long ears and fingers – but I didn't get a good enough look at the others,' she said. 'Frank, how long will it take us to get to Monster World Prison?'

Thanks to the jerky movements of the wheelie bin and the out-cold Sleep Stealer, it took Frank a couple of minutes to balance well enough so he could free his right hand to work the device on his left wrist.

'The signal is r-rubbish,' he said. 'But I took a screenshot of the map earlier, so looking at the distance, and assuming we're moving at about three miles per hour, it should take us . . .' He muttered some calculations under his breath. 'About seventy-seven minutes.'

'That's also assuming we don't meet any hurdles along the way,' said Max. 'This is Monster World, after all.'

'Or any more prisoners,' added Frank.

Grace smiled. 'Well, if we do, we have this brand-new high-security vehicle we can chuck them into. It's just a shame that we can't tell Colonel Hardy we've made progress. Frank, can you call her from your video watch?'

Frank shook his head. 'The signal isn't good enough,' he said. 'But I can post a message and it'll send as soon as we have a connection.'

'Good idea,' said Grace. Then scowling, she added, 'You'd better tell her that our proper video phone was eaten too.'

With Frank concentrating on sending his message while holding a sleepy monster, Kenny using all his might to keep the bin lid closed, and Grace and Max focusing on pushing the strange mode of prisoner transport, none of them took any notice of the flat, square, grey building they passed. It had a shiny golden crown perched on top of it. Nor did they see the little brown donkey and strange-looking bicycle tied to the railings outside . . .

CHAPTER NINE

Beyoncé

'I need to speak to the Monster World Authorities Manager,' said Mr Harris to the security troll sitting behind the desk inside the reception area of the headquarters. 'Now.'

'We don't have a manager,' sneered the troll.

'Then I need the Chief of Operations,' barked Mr Harris.

The troll inspected his yellow fingernail. 'None of those here either.'

'The CEO then,' demanded Mr Harris.

The troll shook his head without making eye contact.

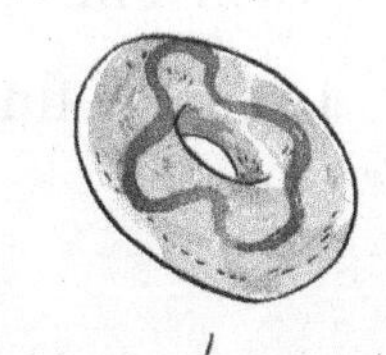

Mr Harris leaned across the desk and hissed, 'Just fetch me the most important person in this building.'

The troll leaned forward, closing the gap between them. 'And who are you exactly?'

The cyclops straightened up. 'I am Senior Field Agent Mr Harris,' he said slowly and crisply.

'So, you're a farmer,' said the troll, uninterested. 'Should've known from your jacket and straw hat.'

'Not those sorts of fields,' snapped Mr Harris. 'I work for the Secret Service. I'm very important!'

The troll narrowed his eyes.

'Listen, if you don't let me through, I will make sure you lose your comfy desk job and get put back on one of those Human World gateways. And trust me, they're not good places for trolls when I'm around,' said Mr Harris menacingly, jabbing a finger towards his mouth.

The troll looked alarmed. 'Fine,' he said grumpily, squishing his bottom further into his comfy chair. 'But if you get in there and start trying to sell them something or ask them to make a monthly donation to your farm, I will remove you myself.'

'I don't have a farm,' Mr Harris mumbled.

The troll picked up the phone and spoke quietly into it, glancing up at the cyclops every few seconds.

'You can go through,' the troll said begrudgingly, replacing the phone. 'Apparently, they know who you are. Eleventh door on the left. Don't touch anything. Wear this at all times.'

As he took the visitor badge from the sulky troll, a wide grin spread across Mr Harris's face. 'They know who I am,' he said slowly. Then he cleared his throat. 'Well, yes, of course they do!' He held his head high and headed confidently towards the double doors by the side of the reception desk. They didn't move, and he banged his head hard.

'Sorry,' said the troll, smirking. 'My bad. I didn't press the release button hard enough.'

Mr Harris pointed to his big angry eye then threateningly at the troll, who slid down in his chair and pushed the release button properly.

Once through, Mr Harris found himself in a corridor, lined with doors on both sides. Some were big, some were small, some were wide, some were impossibly narrow. And all were painted different colours. Some even had glitter on them. The floor was soft matting, fitted together like a jigsaw, like the floor you might find in a soft play centre.

'Well, this is a lot nicer than drab old 10 Downing Street,' he said to himself as he bounced down the corridor to the eleventh door on the left.

The door was medium-sized and painted lime green. It had a yellow handle that looked as if it might glow in the dark. A sign, placed quite near the bottom of the door, read *Important Staff*.

'Good. I'm definitely in the right place,' Mr

Harris said to himself. He cleared his throat and knocked on the door loudly.

'Come in,' said a husky voice from inside.

Mr Harris pushed the door open and stepped inside.

'Hello,' said the husky voice. 'What a pleasure to meet you. Monster World Board Game Champion 1962, I believe?'

'Er, yes, I am . . . him. And I am a Secret Cyclops. I mean, a Secret Service Cyclops. I mean, a Senior Field Farming Cyclops,' Mr Harris stuttered, looking at the blonde figure behind the desk. 'And you're a . . . a . . . cyclops too.'

'Correct, *Senior Field Officer* Mr Harris,' she said, standing up, holding out a chunky, greenish hand that sported several rings and a huge beaded bracelet. 'I'm Beyoncé Kate Venetia Catarina Margarita Gwyneth McDonald, an important member of staff here at the Monster World Authorities. Pleased to meet you.'

'What a beautiful name,' Mr Harris said, shaking her hand.

'Thank you,' Beyoncé replied, fluttering her thick lashes.

'You have a beautiful eye,' Mr Harris whispered.

Beyoncé smiled. 'Thank you. Yours is very . . . big.'

'I'm sorry to break up this over-extended greeting,' snapped a troll with her hair pulled back into a neat ponytail. Her twisted hands, with bright red painted nails, hovered over an old-fashioned typewriter in the corner of the room. 'But we have a meeting in ten minutes. What's your business?'

Mr Harris scowled. 'Neat, rude, demanding. You remind me of a certain colonel,' he muttered then, louder, said, 'and who are you?'

'Miss Patricia Harding,' the troll said, glaring. 'Head Rule-keeping Troll. Not that it's any of your business. Now, what *is* your business?'

Mr Harris glared back. 'Even the name is similar. I wonder if they're related,' he said under his breath. 'I'm here to reassure you that I have the prison break *under control*. All on my own, because I'm so good at my job. I'm the best Senior Field Officer the Human World Secret Service has. You're lucky they've spared me.' He nodded self-importantly, snatching a glance at Beyoncé, who was beaming.

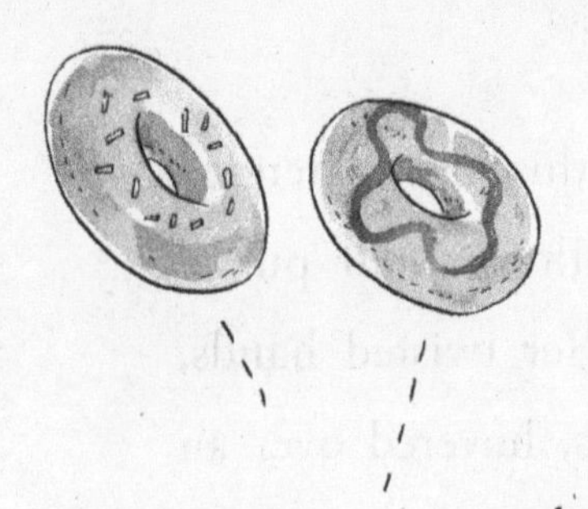

Patricia typed furiously, not once taking her eyes off the cyclops. She whipped the page out of the typewriter and thrust it towards a little creature on the floor that looked a bit like a mop head. A pair of delicate hands emerged from the tangle of hair and took the paper, carrying it lovingly to a large cabinet at the side of the room and filing it immediately.

'Robots,' said Mr Harris knowingly.

'It's not a robot,' hissed Patricia. 'It's a Document Devil. We'd drown in paperwork without them. Now, you say you have this situation under control, so how many of the forty-three monsters have been caught? All of them, I presume, if the situation is *under control*?'

Mr Harris looked from left to right. 'I'll, er, need to call my team for an update.'

'I thought you were doing this *all on your own*?' said Patricia.

'I am,' he spat. 'I have come here, to this office, *all on my own*, to reassure you. So, be reassured.' He turned to Beyoncé and flashed his most charming smile.

'I feel better already!' she said encouragingly, while Patricia typed thunderously in the corner, a queue of Document Devils by her feet.

'Good,' said Mr Harris soothingly to Beyoncé. 'I'll drop back in to debrief once the mission is complete and I have secured my promotion to King of Operations.'

'Oh, yes, please do!' cried Beyoncé.

Mr Harris tipped his hats and thought fleetingly about offering her a small slice of his cake.

'Would you like a . . .' he started. Then he thought better of it and raised his eyebrow jauntily. 'Another handshake before I leave?'

CHAPTER TEN

The Fun Grinch

By the time Grace, Kenny, Frank and Max arrived at the looming gates of Monster World Prison, the monsters inside the bin had tired themselves out and had gone very quiet.

The imposing metal door, which was covered in scratches, was opened by a very small Fun Grinch wearing a power suit with padded shoulders and a pinched waist. Two mean-looking Key Catchers sat on her squared shoulders, their skinny arms folded across their chests. Kenny jumped up and down on top of the bin and waved enthusiastically, but neither of his relations moved a millimetre.

'Dr Delores Darvill. I run this prison,' the Fun Grinch said. 'I assume you are human, with the exception of the Key Catcher, and that you have brought one of my prisoners back. Brandy McNap, I see. The least dangerous monster on the list.'

Max held out his hand. 'I'm Max Hunter. This is Grace, Frank and Kenny. Pleased to meet you. We have actually got seven of your monsters to return. There are six in this bin.'

Dr Darvill raised a thick eyebrow. 'They're very quiet,' she said. Then she screeched, 'GUARDS!'

Within seconds, six trolls wearing police riot gear appeared behind her.

'There's six of the scoundrels in that bin,' she barked. 'Take one each and go directly to the interrogation rooms.' She peered at her own shoulders. 'Kathleen, Kanye, go with them and make sure those rooms are locked. Properly. I will have NO MORE breakouts.'

Frank and Kenny jumped off the bin as the trolls formed an ugly circle round it. The biggest troll, who had a shock of electric-blue hair, counted to three silently and then, like an army major, yelled, 'IN, IN, IN, GO, GO, GO!'

It seemed a bit of an anti-climax when another troll simply flipped the lid open with one finger and let it fall back, revealing the six cross-faced monsters inside.

Each troll plucked a monster out, handcuffed

it and led it towards Dr Darvill. She gave each one a look of pure disgust as they were marched inside the prison. As each passed, she ticked its name off a list she produced from her power suit.

'Number twenty-seven, Penelope Sleighthand, Pickpocket Pixie. As a result of your reckless behaviour, you now have four years added to your prison sentence.

'Number fourteen, Bernard the Barbaric, Road Wrecker. Seven years added.

'Number nine, Charlie John McChomp, Cable Cutter. One year and four months added.

'Number four, Trudy Browning, Toilet Clogger. Forty-four years added.

'Number two, Professor Bob Bright-Light, Sprinkle Sprayer. Life sentence.

'Number thirty-one, Oscar de la Dorito, Tech Taker. One week and three hours added.'

'Dr Darvill?' Grace said as the last prisoner disappeared into the shadowy prison. 'The Tech

Taker has actually eaten my video phone. I don't suppose there's a way of getting it back, is there?'

Dr Darvill scrunched up her nose. 'Why would you want it back when it's been in a Tech Taker? You'll never get the tangy cheese smell out of it.'

'I don't really want it back now you've said that, but it's the best way to communicate with our team and Colonel Hardy,' said Grace.

'As you wish,' said Dr Darvill. 'Give us an hour or so and I'll send it back to you by messenger bat. If I can get one to agree to take it . . .'

'Thank you, that'd be great,' said Grace, wondering if a messenger bat was what she thought it was – a Monster World version of a messenger pigeon.

Dr Darvill nodded. 'I might have more news for you by then, if any of the rogues you've brought back have talked during their interrogations.'

Before she closed the door, Frank piped up, 'Doctor? What would you like me to do with Brandy McNap?'

The formidable Fun Grinch frowned. 'Leave him by the door. I'll get a security troll to fetch him later.' Then she gave a curt nod and closed the door.

Frank looked troubled as he placed the Sleep Stealer gently on the doormat. 'He's quite sweet,' he said. 'Can't we just take him with us, Dad?'

'Not really, Frank – he's a prisoner, however sweet he is,' said Max. 'And trust me, you'll never have a good night's sleep again if you keep him. They're absolute rascals overnight.'

Frank gave Brandy McNap a pat on the head.

At the end of the prison driveway, Grace turned to Frank. 'Which way to the Forest of Fiends?'

'We need to go right. We have to get over B-Brutal Bridge first. Lucky us,' he said nervously.

'Wow, that sounds like fun. Next you'll be telling me that trolls live under it!' Grace laughed.

'They do, actually,' said Max, nodding. 'But not the ones who like guarding gates and following careers in security, unfortunately.'

'Oh, well, baking powder and cakes at the ready,' Grace said cheerily, plunging her hand into her rucksack.

Brutal Bridge was exactly how Grace had imagined it. Big and rickety, with pieces of wood missing and no rail to hold on to. Moss clung to its edges, while a low, silvery mist swirled eerily around it, above the murky river that whooshed underneath it.

Frank held his fork out in front of him. His other hand clutched a pot of baking powder.

'Two minutes and we'll be on the other side,' said Max, squeezing Frank's shoulder reassuringly.

'Or not,' came a gruff voice. The ground beneath them trembled as a large shape emerged from the mist.

'Max Hunter. We meet again.'

CHAPTER ELEVEN

Dirk the Destroyer

A bulky creature made its way up the river bank from beneath the bridge. As it moved closer to them, Grace could see it wore a Monster World Prison jumpsuit. She noticed that some of the fabric from the legs was missing, but quickly realised that it was wrapped around the monster's boulder-like head as a bandana, while other scraps had been tied round its wrists like cuffs. It might have been a more threatening look had the remaining material not looked like a very short playsuit that a member of a girl band might wear.

What did make the creature more scary, however, were the powerful muscles straining in its arms and legs. It would have been no surprise if it could pick up a minibus with one hand. It had enormous feet, with stocky toes, most of which had thick, crooked, dirty nails. One large toe, however, sported a vicious-looking claw, like those found on the T-Rex back at the museum.

'Brian Smith, Freak-footed Troll,' Max breathed. 'I didn't see your name on the list.'

'That's because I've changed it,' bellowed the creature. 'I fancied something a little more in keeping with my nature. I'm Dirk now . . . Dirk the Destroyer!'

'Wow, really?' said Max, looking more puzzled than concerned. 'Dirk?'

'THE DESTROYER!' yelled Dirk. 'Don't upset me, Max Hunter, or I'll take your other arm.'

Grace gasped and Frank clamped his hand over his mouth in horror. His fork missed his eye by millimetres. Kenny slipped down Grace's arm and into her pocket.

Max plunged his hand into his pocket, pulled out a tub of baking powder and threw it. As it spiralled through the air, Dirk raised one leg like a professional kickboxer. His toe-claw cut through the tub like paper, spraying baking powder in the opposite direction.

'Have you forgotten what I'm capable of?' said Dirk, taking a step towards Max. The ground moved under Grace and Frank's feet.

'No, I haven't,' said Max firmly. 'Now, whether you like it or not, we have to take you in.'

Dirk threw his head back and laughed. 'Take me in! And how are you going to do that? With these two tiny helpers?'

Grace scowled and tightened her grip on her baking powder.

Dirk suddenly stopped laughing and hissed, 'Get onto the bridge.' He flexed his toe, pushing the jagged claw out another inch.

Max shot Grace and Frank a look and gestured for them to step onto the bridge. Grace went first, then Frank, their tubs of baking powder concealed in their hands. Max followed them, with Dirk behind him. The bridge wobbled and creaked.

'Stop here!' Dirk bellowed. 'We're going to play a game.'

They stopped and turned round to face him.

'All sorts of things live in this water,' he said, gesturing to the murky brown river. 'Lots of them have very pointy teeth and haven't had their dinner yet. Now, you're all going to jump in and try to swim to the other side. If you don't get eaten, I'll let you go. If you do get eaten – well, then you won't be going anywhere.' He chuckled.

'That's not a very fair game,' said Grace angrily, trying to get the lid off her baking powder using her thumb.

'Oh well, never mind,' said Dirk. 'Now, before you all practise your dives, chuck in those tubs you're trying to hide in your tiny, weak hands. You've seen what I can do with my feet.'

'I can't s-swim,' said Frank, his fork shaking.

Dirk shrugged. 'At least it'll be quick for you then, Curly. Now, throw the tubs in.'

'We are not going to throw anything in, least of all ourselves,' said Max.

'Throw. Them. In,' spat Dirk, raising one of his hideous feet.

As Grace and Frank reluctantly hung their baking powder over the side of the bridge, the wooden planks beneath their feet began to tremble. Grace could hear footsteps on the crooked walkway, but the air above the bridge was misty, so she couldn't make out who, or what, was responsible.

Dirk must have detected the movement too. He stood very still, claw flexed.

As the stomping came closer, Grace was able to make out a large figure striding purposefully towards them.

Dirk grinned grotesquely. 'That'll be my sister, Barb, coming to give me a hand with the reluctant swimmers.'

'Does he have a sister?' Grace whispered to Max.

Max's shoulders sagged. 'Yes, unfortunately he does. And she's got an extra lethal toe on each foot.'

CHAPTER TWELVE

Accidental Rescue

'If you had just jumped in, you wouldn't be facing two of us,' said Dirk.

'But then we'd have been eaten,' snapped Grace.

'You're going to be eaten anyway,' said Dirk cheerfully. 'In fact, let's speed this process up.' He raised a burly leg and pulled it back, ready to kick out at Max.

Just then, the figure loomed out of the mist. It was looking around, rather frantically. It walked with such determination that it bowled straight into Dirk and sent him flying over the side of the bridge into the shadowy water. There was a frenzy of movement at the surface, as fins and scales and teeth flashed through the water and foam.

'Mr Harris!' yelled Grace.

The cyclops stopped suddenly and focused.

'Doughnut Lady? Oh no, Shrimp Boy too. And one of the dads. How?' he spluttered. 'How are you here? It's so misty, I thought you were a collection of ugly Bridge-dwelling Goblins. Who did I knock in? I think it had prison clothes on, so I assume it's no real loss?'

Max cleared his throat. 'I think you probably just saved our lives, Mr Harris.'

The cyclops raised his eyebrow.

'That Freak-footed T-Troll was trying to make us jump into the water,' said Frank. 'And he's the reason Dad lost his arm years ago!'

'Well, then,' said Mr Harris, puffing out his chest. 'I have no doubt that I did, indeed, save your lives. Once again.

You're so clueless and haphazard. And I really am very good at life-saving. Probably just as good as a King of Operations would be, in actual fact. Anyway, why are you here on this bridge?'

The water swirled beneath them, the odd pointed fin and sharp tooth emerging from the surface.

'Shall we get off this bridge, then talk?' asked Grace, ushering Mr Harris back along the way they had come.

Once they were safely away from the rickety crossing, Mr Harris hurried over to Betsy and his bicycle and untethered them from a tree by the side of the road. It had curious circular leaves.

'So, why are you here?' he called back.

'Why do you have a donkey?' asked Grace. 'I knew I heard a hee-haw when we were on the video call!'

'Answer my question first, Doughnut Lady,' Mr Harris chided.

Grace frowned. 'We've just

returned seven prisoners to Monster World Prison. You know, as part of the mission you're refusing to help with,' she said.

'I think you'll find *I* just caught the most dangerous monster,' said Mr Harris, grinning proudly.

'You didn't catch him! You walked into him because you weren't looking where you were going, and knocked him into the river, which is infested with goodness knows what. It was a fluke!' replied Grace.

The cyclops glared. 'I knew exactly what I was doing. It just so happened that at the time you needed me to rescue you *again*, I was also checking the bridge to see if it would be strong enough to hold my transportation.'

'You said you thought we were ugly Bridge-dwelling Goblins,' Frank interjected quietly, his fork still held out in front of him defensively.

'Easy mistake to make,' muttered Mr Harris.

'But I knew it was you. I could hear Doughnut Lady's unmistakable whine.'

Grace was about to ask again why Mr Harris had a donkey, as well as an ancient bicycle, when her gaze was drawn upwards to the sound of strong wings beating above their heads.

'Urgh, a Giant Bat!' cried Mr Harris. 'Vermin! Explode it now before it swoops down and kills you!'

The bat seemed angry. Its face was wrinkled into an ugly frown and its spiky teeth were bared. As it got closer, Grace could see it was wearing a black and white Monster World Prison neckerchief and it was holding a brown envelope in its clawed feet.

'It's the messenger bat from the prison!' she exclaimed. She waved at it and shouted, 'You found us! Well done!'

The bat looked even angrier. It plunged downwards before letting go of the envelope it was holding. It landed with a thump on top of Grace's head.

'Ouch!' she cried.

Mr Harris burst into raucous laughter. Kenny immediately leapt onto her head and began to rub the sore spot with one hand, using the other to shake his minute fist at the grumpy, winged messenger.

The bat gave a short, sharp hiss and flapped off, chaotically, into the distance.

Grace rubbed her head, where a lump was

forming, then tore the envelope open.

'My video phone!' she said. 'Wow. Dr Darvill was right – it really smells.'

Mr Harris sniffed the air and recoiled. 'Oh, the cheesiness,' he spluttered. 'The mustiness, the funky tang! A Tech Taker's had that.'

Grace rolled her eyes and wiped the phone as best she could with a tissue Kenny had handed her. She switched it on.

'Oh no!' she said. 'There are seventeen missed calls and loads of messages coming through. We missed the last one literally four minutes ago. Something must have happened. Mr Harris, have you missed any calls? Have you had an update?'

The cyclops looked away and shook his head. 'No calls or updates for me,' he said.

'Are you sure?' asked Max. 'Could you check your video phone?'

Mr Harris fumbled in his pocket, drew out the device and glanced at it for a millisecond. 'Nothing. All very quiet and boring.'

Grace narrowed her eyes. 'Can I see?'

'No,' snapped Mr Harris. 'Nosy Doughnut Lady.'

Grace leapt forward and snatched it out of his beefy fist.

'Mr Harris,' she said in disbelief. 'You've switched it off!'

'No, I haven't!' he said. 'It . . . it ran out of battery!'

'But the batteries on these devices last for over a week,' said Frank.

Grace pushed the 'on' button. Beep after beep after beep chimed through.

'Well, would you look at that,' she said, turning the screen towards Mr Harris. 'Seventeen missed calls and lots of messages.'

'What a coincidence!' he exclaimed, bustling towards his bike and donkey. 'Right, shall we get on with this important mission? I believe there are a lot more prisoners to catch and I won't have my team slacking!'

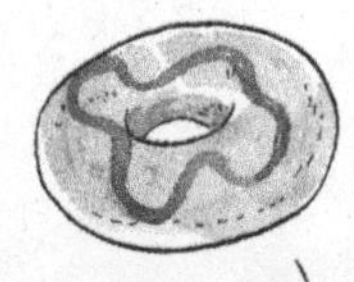

CHAPTER THIRTEEN

But He's Dead!

As fourteen of the missed calls on their phones were from Eamon, Grace called her dad back straight away.

Danni answered immediately. 'Grace! Thank goodness! What happened? Why weren't you answering? And where's Mr Harris? Did you find him? He hasn't been answering his phone either!' She sounded frantic.

'My video phone got eaten by an escaped monster,' said Grace. 'But I've got it back now. Mr Harris had switched his off . . . don't ask. Anyway, how come you're answering Dad's phone?'

'It all got a bit chaotic here,' said Danni, looking relieved to see her little sister unscathed. 'Mum and Dad have gone to catch some monster prisoners near the Natural History Museum. They're causing havoc, apparently.'

'They've gone together?' asked Grace, her tummy somersaulting nervously as she thought of the last time they had gone monster-hunting as a pair. That trip had seen them transported to Monster World in Mr Harris's gullet, not to be seen again for two years.

'Don't worry, they'll be fine,' Danni said softly.

'Why haven't they taken the video phone?' asked Grace.

'They left it with me for when you called back,' Danni replied. 'They've got their mobiles with them. I'm under strict instructions to phone them as soon as I know you haven't been eaten by a rogue monster.'

'Okay, you'd better let

them know,' said Grace. 'Dan, please tell them to be careful.'

'I will. And they'll tell me to tell you the same thing,' her sister said, smiling. 'Just before you go though, the reason I was calling you . . .'

Grace nodded.

'The guards at Monster World Prison have managed to get some information out of the prisoners you returned,' said Danni, her tone serious. 'Several of them have admitted they were helped to escape.'

Grace gasped. 'By who?'

'None of them will say,' Danni replied. 'But there's something else . . .'

'Go on,' said Grace.

'They've all said the same thing about where they were going,' said Danni. 'They've all said they were going to find their leader, Neville Harris.'

Grace frowned as she thought back to the explosive scenes at 10 Downing Street,

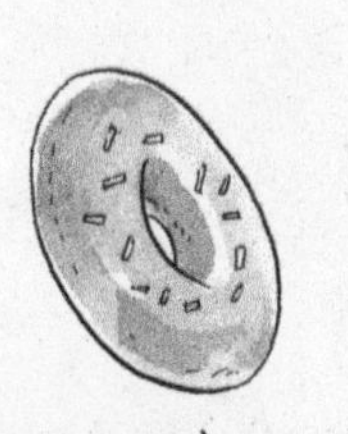

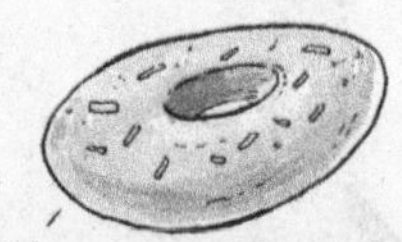

when she, Frank and Mr Harris had saved the Prime Minister and destroyed Neville, Mr Harris's evil grandfather.

'But he's dead,' she said.

'What if he isn't, Grace?' said Danni, her eyes full of concern. 'What if they know something we don't?'

'Well, then we're in big trouble,' Grace replied. 'We need to track down more prisoners and ask them a lot of questions. We need to know if he's still alive. Have you checked the Monster Scanner?'

'Not yet. I only got the information just before you called,' said Danni, shaking her head. 'I'll check now and call you back, okay? Oh for goodness' sake, three customers have just walked in. I'll serve them, then check, then call you back! Got to go. Sis, be careful. Please.'

As the screen went blank, Grace became aware of someone close behind her.

'Who might still be alive?' asked Mr Harris, his arms folded across his chest.

Frank and Max had turned towards her too, and Kenny had pulled himself out of her pocket and onto her shoulder.

Grace took a deep breath. 'Neville,' she said. 'It's possible that the monsters had help to escape the prison so they could go and find him. We may not have destroyed him after all.'

CHAPTER FOURTEEN

Eye-Spy Wood

'Nonsense!' scoffed Mr Harris. 'I watched that leathery old reptile disintegrate into dust.'

'Perhaps he can regenerate?' said Grace, thinking out loud. 'Like you can. I hadn't thought about it before, because it's so unusual in monsters. I thought you were unique.'

'I AM UNIQUE! He can't do it. I'm much better than him,' declared the cyclops.

'This is not the right time for an ego trip, Mr Harris,' said Grace. 'We need to find out as quickly as possible if there's any chance he's alive.'

'We must t-track down the rest of the escaped monsters so they can be questioned,' added Frank.

'Well, it's going to have to be on the way to find my mother,' said Mr Harris. 'You interrupted my personal mission with your ridiculous prison breakout, so mine takes priority.'

'This route to the Forest of Fiends is off the beaten track,' said Max. 'If the prisoners are going to be hiding anywhere, I bet some will be here. So we can join the missions for the time being, Mr Harris. But we need to get going. At least the bridge should be easier to cross without Brian – I mean, Dirk – lurking under it.'

Apart from one hairy moment, when Mr Harris jumped up and down to prove the bridge was safe, and two wide wooden slats just in front of Betsy broke in half and fell into the water, the crossing was uneventful.

The other side revealed an unmade path with lots of signs saying *KEEP OFF THE GRASS – A.G. TERRITORY.*

'A.G. territory?' Grace questioned.

'Call yourself a monster hunter?' scoffed Mr Harris. 'Ankle Grabber territory.'

Max agreed. 'He's right. Ferocious little things. They're hand-shaped and incredibly strong. They come out of nowhere, grab your ankles and won't let go. Once they've latched on, they retreat back into the ground so there's almost no way of prising them off. Sometimes they hang on for days on end. Keep to the path, everyone.'

'Where does this take us, Frank?' Grace asked.

Frank consulted his wrist. 'This p-path goes to Eye-Spy Wood,' he said, his brow furrowed with unease.

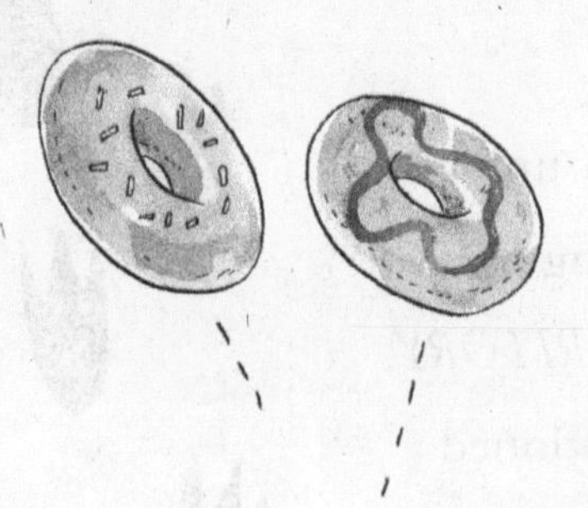

'OH! I LOVE THAT PLACE!' said Mr Harris, immediately animated. 'Full of hidden treehouses from the time of the Great Monster Revolt. Some even have skeletons in. Magical.'

'Treehouses sound like good hiding places,' said Grace.

Kenny, who was keeping lookout from beside Grace's ear, nodded in agreement then pointed further along the path.

Grace could see a flare of black and white up ahead, on the grass. As they got closer, she made out a pointy-nosed goblin with huge ears, lying on its side in the grass. It had its head propped up on its hand and it was picking daisy-like flowers with the other, then eating them. The legs of its jumpsuit were torn, and Grace could just make out earthy fingers, like tree roots, clamped round one of the goblin's ankles.

'What's your name?' asked Max.

The goblin looked bored. 'Bruce,' he said.

'Do you have a surname?' asked Frank politely, scanning the wanted list.

'Goblin,' said the goblin patronisingly.

'Oh, yes, here you are,' said Frank. 'Number Five. Bruce Archibald Goblin. Large-eared Goblin. Serving thirty-three days and twenty-seven minutes for the theft of a fancy rat.'

'Stupid rat,' muttered Bruce. 'Wasn't even that fancy.'

'Well, consider yourself arrested by me, Senior Field Officer slash nearly King of Operations!' barked Mr Harris. 'You do not have to say anything, but anything you do say –'

'Shhh!' said Grace to the cyclops, facing the goblin. 'How did you escape?'

'Who's asking?' sneered Bruce.

'We are, and you might as well tell us because we'll be returning you to prison. If you help us, we might be able to help you when it comes to Dr Darvill extending your sentence,' said Grace firmly.

The goblin laughed nastily. 'She doesn't scare me. She's surprisingly helpful . . . for the head of a prison.'

Grace felt the hairs on her arms stand up. 'What do you mean, helpful?'

'No comment,' said Bruce.

'Did she help you escape?' asked Max.

'No comment,' said the goblin again.

'W-What were you going to do once you were out?' asked Frank.

'I want my lawyer,' snapped Bruce.

'Okay, let's not waste any more time here,' said Mr Harris. 'I'm hungry and Bruce is boring.'

'How are we going to get the Ankle Grabber off him without getting grabbed ourselves?' questioned Grace.

Mr Harris rolled his eye. 'Your IQ must be shockingly low. We leave him here. Obviously. An Ankle Grabber that thick isn't going to let go anytime soon. Bruce is in for the long haul!'

'Max?' said Grace. 'Do you think he's right?'

'Yes, I think so,' Max replied. 'We'll call it in and get someone from the prison, with the proper equipment, to come and fetch him.'

'Outrageous! Leaving me here at the mercy of the elements and the Ankle Grabbers!' shouted Bruce behind them.

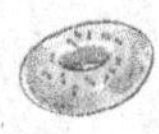

The path led into a dense woodland. Thousands of trees of all shapes and sizes were packed together, creating an enclosed, shadowy space.

'Look at this tree!' said Grace, moving towards a strange sapling with sinewy silver branches and tiny gold leaves shaped like musical notes.

'DO NOT touch that tree!' bellowed Mr Harris, shaking his head. 'Doughnut Lady, you have so much to learn. Touch that thing and it'll start singing. And never stop. They are screechy and loud and awful. Do. Not. Do. It.'

Grace pulled her hand back. The tree shook

angrily, thrusting its branches towards Mr Harris as though it was telling him off.

'Oh my goblins,' Frank piped up from behind them. His fork was pointing up. 'Look.'

Grace looked up and her eyes widened. Hundreds of treehouses perched in the branches above them. Some huge ones sat on top of quite small trees, and other, crooked ones, nestled among branches so they were barely visible. One was a replica of Buckingham Palace. The tree it was plonked on top of was short and stocky, as though it had been pushed down by the weight of the treehouse.

'Oh my word,' Grace whispered. 'That's a lot of hiding places.'

'We need to do something to draw them out,' said Max, gazing upwards in awe.

'No!' moaned Mr Harris. 'I'm hungry! Let's draw them out after snacks.'

Grace's eyes lit up. 'That's an excellent idea!' she cried.

'What? Why are you agreeing with me?' he said gruffly.

'Because monsters love cakes! And we have lots of those!' she said excitedly. 'Who fancies a picnic?'

CHAPTER FIFTEEN

Come Out, Come Out, Wherever You Are!

They found a clearing and a patch of grass among a dense tangle of trees, below the little wooden treehouses woven throughout the branches all around them. Mr Harris insisted on checking the trees for any that might sing, shout or recite rude limericks before he chose a dead sapling to tether Betsy and his bicycle to. They spread out a cloth that some of the explosive muffins from the bakery had been wrapped in, and sat down.

'Mmm, let's get out our yummy human cakes,' said Grace loudly and clearly, hoping that ears of many colours, shapes and sizes might perk up in their hiding places.

Frank glanced round nervously and said, 'I h-hope Johnny Big-Hands isn't here. I'm not sure we're ready for a Non-compliant G-giant.'

'Don't worry, Frank, we'll find a way to deal with whatever or whoever is here. We're Hunters!' Max replied quietly, before turning and saying in a booming voice, 'So many cakes to choose from!'

They pulled cookies, muffins, scones, pastries, doughnuts, tarts, choux buns and fruit pies out of their rucksacks. All had been expertly spiked with far too much baking powder by Danni and Louisa.

Mr Harris shook his head. 'What a shocking waste,' he said, reaching for a doughnut covered in multi-coloured sprinkles.

Grace slapped his massive hand. 'Do not eat any! You will explode, and goodness only knows where you'll go, since we're already in Monster World.'

'Wherever it was, it'd be quieter and less bossy than here,' he mumbled. Then he scowled and gestured angrily to the cakes. 'What do I get to eat if all these are off limits? I probably wouldn't even explode, I'm so strong and powerful. I'll just have one . . .' His chunky fingers hovered over a cinnamon bun.

Once again, Grace knocked his hand back. 'No! Eat your safe cake. Is it still in that bag?' She grimaced.

Mr Harris glanced at his bag for life. 'I'm saving that.'

'For when? It must be an absolute mess by now. You're probably best eating it while it's still sort of edible,' said Grace.

'I'm saving it for a special occasion!' snapped the cyclops. 'I may even decide to share it with someone.'

Grace raised her eyebrows. 'Share it? You? With whom?' she said in disbelief. 'Oh, do you mean with your mum? That's actually quite sweet of you.'

Mr Harris scowled. 'More questions. Of course. Because nosy Doughnut Lady must stick her pointy beak into everybody's business. Not that it has anything to do with you, but I didn't mean my mother. I met a very charming and terribly important cyclops earlier today. I could tell immediately that she has outstanding taste and would truly appreciate a cake of that standard. Not like you greedy cake-hoggers.'

'She?' said Grace, smiling.

Kenny leaned forward excitedly, while Max and Frank grinned from the other side of the cloth.

'Mr Harris! Has a lady cyclops taken your fancy?' said Grace, eyes bright with mischief.

The cyclops looked disgusted. 'What a horribly undignified thing to say,' he replied. 'But not surprising coming from you. She is a professional contact. Keep it corporate, Doughnut Lady.'

'What's her n-name?' asked Frank.

Mr Harris straightened his shoulders. 'She is a very important member of staff at the Monster World Authorities Headquarters – Miss Beyoncé Kate Venetia Catarina Margarita Gwyneth McDonald,' he said seriously.

Grace snorted with laughter but, seeing the cyclops's furious glare, coughed. 'Ahem. What a lovely name.'

Suddenly, Kenny began to jump up and down, pointing towards the undergrowth.

A pair of beady green eyes stared intently at the cakes.

Kenny pointed frantically in the other direction.

A furry brown snout sniffed the air from between two big heart-shaped leaves.

Grace scanned the edge of the clearing and the treehouses directly above. She saw paws and claws, eyes and ears, bottoms and elbows, tails and horns. And lots of black and white jump-suits.

'We're s-surrounded,' whispered Frank.

'Don't worry, son,' Max said firmly. 'Assertiveness is best in these situations. Trust me, I've been here before. While they're distracted, call Dr Darvill and tell her we need back-up.'

'Do we trust her, though? After what the goblin said? What if she's the one who's been helping the monsters escape?' said Grace quietly.

'I'm not sure there's anyone else who could get here quickly enough,' said Max.

Mr Harris cleared his throat. 'I could contact Miss McDonald. She's very important.'

Max nodded slowly. 'Yes, okay, you call your contact, Mr Harris. And Grace, Frank, contact Colonel Hardy. Tell her we have some concerns about Dr Darvill that we need to iron out before we can call her directly.'

Max stood up and cleared his throat. 'We can see you,' he said confidently. 'We have stolen these cakes from Human World, so if you want some you're going to have to queue sensibly.'

'Who are you?' came a scratchy voice from a treehouse above them.

'We are Lesser-known Human-faced Trolls,' said Max sincerely. 'We're hiding out in these woods because we don't want to be taken to

Monster World Prison for possession of illegal fondant fancies.'

A murmur of agreement and support washed through the trees and bushes. One by one, monsters of various shapes and sizes began to emerge.

'Queue here, please,' said Max, indicating a space to the side of the cloth.

The monsters happily formed a neat line. Many of them craned their necks to see what treats were on offer; some rubbed their hands together in glee; and many dribbled freely onto the mossy ground. None seemed to find the situation even slightly suspicious.

Max turned away from the line and said under his breath, 'Make those calls. I've counted fourteen so far, and they're still coming.'

CHAPTER SIXTEEN

Monster Round-up

After the calls had been made, Grace announced that the cake giveaway would happen in fifteen minutes. None of the monsters questioned the delay; all stayed neatly in line.

'Blow them up, Doughnut Lady. It's what you used to do to me all the time,' said Mr Harris.

'And you just kept coming back,' said Grace, chuckling.

'Given their remarkably good behaviour, it seems a bit unreasonable to blow them up. Are we agreed that we'll wait for back-up and then they can be returned to prison?' said Max quietly.

Grace, Frank and Kenny nodded.

Mr Harris tutted loudly. 'They're monsters. One will kick off before long. Although it's quite clear they've only got about four brain cells between them. Look at them, waiting for their cake! Who waits for cake?' he scoffed, plunging his hand into his bag for life.

'Not now!' Grace said, gritting her teeth. 'They'll wonder why you can have your cake if they can't have theirs. We don't want to cause any unrest.'

'Fun hoover,' muttered Mr Harris, drawing his hand out of the bag and licking his fingers.

'While we wait for b-back-up,' Frank said, leaning in, 'we can question some of them. Maybe we'll get more information about Dr D-Darvill.'

'Let's do it in pairs,' said Grace. 'Just in case.'

'Come on, Frank,' said Max. 'Let's go and talk to the Tree Hugger – they're well known for being friendly and calm.'

'Looks like you've bagged the best partner,

Doughnut Lady,' said Mr Harris. 'I mean me, by the way, not the stick insect on your shoulder.'

'Lucky me,' said Grace. 'Right, who shall we speak to? Is that a Chatterbox Brownie? She will be more than happy to tell us EVERYTHING she knows! We need to play a bit dumb, though, to get her talking.'

'That won't be a problem for you,' said Mr Harris, then he scowled. 'Last Chatterbox Brownie I came across tasted of soap. I assumed it would taste of brownies. Colossal disappointment.'

Grace pointed her finger at the cyclops. 'Do NOT eat her. If you feel even remotely monster-eaty, you must walk away, okay?'

Mr Harris glared and strode towards the Chatterbox Brownie, who was tapping the monster in front of her on the shoulder enthusiastically.

'Hi,' said Grace, smiling. 'Can I ask a quick question?'

'Ooh, yes!' cried the Brownie. 'I love questions!'

'Great!' said Grace as Mr Harris sighed irritably behind her. She lowered her voice. 'I just wondered why you're all wearing matching jumpsuits. Have you all come from the same place?'

The Brownie frowned. 'Oh, well, yes. I'm not very proud to say that we all came from Monster World Prison.'

Grace fake-gasped.

'Surely not?' said Mr Harris sarcastically.

'None of us here did anything very bad,' the Brownie said quickly. 'For example, all I did was make a yeti break his vow of silence after forty-nine years. I didn't even mean to.'

'Did he tell you to shush?' said Mr Harris rudely.

'Yes!' exclaimed the Brownie. 'How did you know? Did you read the story in the *Monster World Times*?'

Before Mr Harris could say anything, Grace interrupted. 'That doesn't sound bad at all. So, why are you all here? Were you all released on the same day?'

The Brownie shook her head and looked ashamed. 'Not released, really. We had help to leave . . . well, escape. I know, I know, it sounds terrible!' she said pleadingly. 'But we don't need to be in prison. She told us that, if we wanted

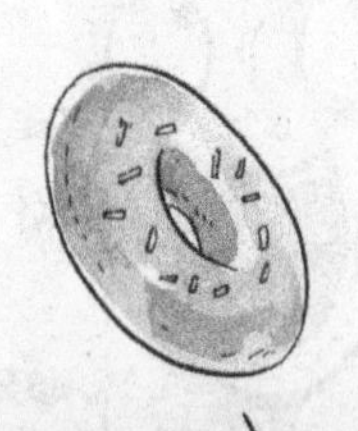

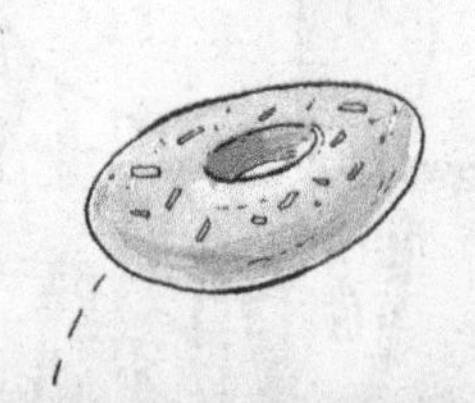

to, we could get out and go to a special place – the happiness hub, she called it – with this wonderful, strong leader who would help us be better monsters. So we sort of had permission . . .'

'She?' asked Grace, her heart beating fast. 'Who's *she*? And do you know anything about the leader she mentioned? It all sounds very interesting.'

'The lady who works at the prison. She seemed a little strict at first, but she's a great role model and teacher,' said the Chatterbox Brownie fondly. 'I don't know much about the leader, though. Oh! Some of the other monsters knew about him already . . .'

Grace raised her eyebrows, trying to take everything in. 'The lady who works at the prison? Do you mean Dr –' Grace was interrupted by a commotion in the trees behind them.

'GET ON THE GROUND! EVERYONE GET ON THE GROUND!' came a deafening screech. A sizeable figure, wearing full riot gear, leather gloves and steel-capped boots, and holding a shield, erupted out of the bushes. Its head was encased in a shiny black helmet, at the back of which was a sea of long blonde hair. A single aqua-blue eye stared meanly out of the clear visor at the front.

'Miss Beyoncé Kate Venetia Catarina Margarita Gwyneth McDonald?' whispered Mr Harris, straightening his hats and pulling down his scruffy tweed jacket.

The blue eye softened and a leather glove waved. 'Senior Field Officer Mr Harris!' said the cyclops in a soft, husky voice. 'Give me a minute!'

Mr Harris nodded obediently.

Beyoncé shook her shield intimidatingly and yelled, 'GET DOWN NOW! YOU'RE BUSTED! YOU'RE ON YOUR WAY BACK TO MONSTER WORLD PRISON, RIGHT NOW!' She breathed heavily through her nostrils as the monsters dropped onto their bellies, some of them openly moaning about being caught before they'd had cake.

‘TEAM!’ she shrieked. ‘CUFF THEM!’

A dozen more riot officer monsters scuttled out of the trees, brandishing handcuffs.

Grace noticed that Mr Harris seemed rather shell-shocked.

‘Is this the cyclops you took a fancy to?’ she asked mischievously. ‘She’s very stern.’

Mr Harris continued to stare, open-mouthed, at Beyoncé and said nothing.

As the officers handcuffed the monsters, Beyoncé walked over to them, unzipping her riot jacket, revealing a smart blouse underneath. She lifted her helmet off her head and shook out her long golden locks.

‘We came as soon as we could,’ she said sweetly.

Mr Harris said nothing but his wide mouth hung slightly open.

‘Pleased to meet you,’ Beyoncé said, holding her chunky hand out towards Grace, who took it politely.

‘And you,’ said Grace. ‘Mr Harris mentioned seeing you earlier.’

‘Did he now?’ Beyoncé giggled. ‘Well, this little distraction he came up with stopped me eating my lunch, so I hope you don’t mind if I take one of your delicious cakes?’

CHAPTER SEVENTEEN

The Plot Thickens

The mention of the explosive cakes jolted Mr Harris out of his trance. He leapt in front of Beyoncé, throwing himself on top of the cloth, squashing all the pastries, muffins and buns. There was uproar from the handcuffed monsters. Beyoncé frowned.

'These are not safe!' cried Mr Harris. 'You'll explode if you eat these! Ask her! It's all her doing!' He pointed accusingly at Grace.

Grace glared at him. 'These are our secret weapons,' she said to Beyoncé. Then she gestured at Mr Harris, who was staring intently at his own hand, which was covered in icing. 'This mess is his clumsy way of trying to protect you. Mr Harris! Do NOT lick your hand!'

Beyoncé's face relaxed. 'Oh, I see. But that's a shame. I really am hungry.'

'That's not a problem,' said Grace. 'I'm sure Mr Harris will share his un-dangerous cake with you. No secret ingredient in that one! It's in the blue bag for life just there.'

'Ooh!' squealed Beyoncé. 'That sounds wonderful!'

Mr Harris glowered at Grace. As Beyoncé made her way towards the bag, he leaned in and hissed, 'I hadn't decided if I wanted to share my celebration and jubilation cake, Doughnut Lady!'

'It would be very rude not to,' Grace replied. 'And look how much she's enjoying it!'

Mr Harris twisted round and stared at Beyoncé in horror.

'This is delicious,' she said, in between handfuls of sponge and buttercream. 'Thank you so much for giving it to me.'

'I did not give –' he started.

Kenny leapt from Grace's shoulder and pincered the cyclops's lips shut with his wiry fingers.

'You did not give . . . it to anyone else! That's right, Mr Harris!' Grace improvised. 'You must be very special, Miss McDonald. He doesn't usually share his cakes.'

Beyoncé fluttered her eyelashes and chuckled, then held the bag up and emptied the remainder of its contents into her expansive mouth.

A muffled moan came from behind Kenny's fingers.

'They're all cuffed, ma'am,' said a small, round monster with pointy ears. He bowed as the cyclops turned to him.

'Thank you, Giles. Return them all directly to Dr Darvill at Monster World Prison immediately,' Beyoncé said.

'As you wish, ma'am,' said Giles, bowing over and over again as he walked backwards away from her.

'I wish I got that sort of respect from my team,' Mr Harris mumbled, his mouth now unclamped and Kenny safely in Grace's pocket.

Grace shot him a look. 'Miss McDonald, about Dr Darvill . . . is she trustworthy?'

Beyoncé nodded. 'She's always been very reliable. This is the first prison break on her watch,' she said. Then she leaned forward and

whispered, 'Personally, I suspect she was playing chess and got distracted. She makes the prisoners hold tournaments, she's so obsessed with it. I mean, we all love board games, but I'm more of a snakes and ladders girl myself.'

Mr Harris's eye brightened. 'An excellent choice! I was once gifted a rare version of snakes and ladders by the Prime Minister in Human World. That's how important I am.'

'You should use it to practise. Even I've beaten you at snakes and ladders,' Grace said cheerfully.

Mr Harris growled under his breath.

'I'll challenge you next if you're easy to beat!' said Beyoncé, before turning back to Grace. 'Why do you ask about Dr Darvill?'

'It's just that a few of the prisoners have said they had help to escape. It sounds like it was an inside job,' said Grace.

'Add that Poo Shuffler over there to the list,' said Max, joining them with Frank. 'He said they were given access cards and keys and told when to make a run for it. He won't say who helped, but he did accidentally say it was a she.'

'The Chatterbox Brownie said the same – she said someone who is a little strict but is a good role model and teacher. She also mentioned going to find a special place with a strong leader,' said Grace.

'That's interesting,' said Max. He addressed Beyoncé. 'We'll come back to the prison with you, Miss McDonald. There's clearly something that needs investigating.'

Mr Harris looked torn. 'Obviously, as the officer in charge of this mission, I should come with you, but I have another important, top-secret mission to attend to. If you just wait here for a few hours, I'll be back as quickly as possible and we can all go together.'

'We can't just wait here for a few hours!' said Grace. 'Why don't Frank and I come with you, and Max can go with Miss McDonald? We'll find your . . . er . . . secret location more quickly if it's the three of us and Kenny, especially with Frank's technical skills. Then we can all meet back at the prison.'

'You'll slow me down!' moaned Mr Harris.

'I think it's the bike and the donkey that are more likely to slow you down,' Grace retorted.

'Is that noble steed yours?' cried Beyoncé. 'I thought one of the prisoners had stolen it! How grand! My goodness, you must be important to have your own cavalry!'

Mr Harris grinned in delight and pushed his straw hat, which was still over his normal hat, to a jaunty angle.

'Oh my goblins, they're all as mad as each other,' Frank whispered.

'Let's just get him reunited with his mum, have a cup of tea and then get back to Monster World Prison as quickly as possible so we can find out what's been going on,' Grace said. 'I want to know what Dr Darvill has been up to.'

CHAPTER EIGHTEEN

A Worrying Discovery

Grace, Kenny, Frank and Mr Harris, with Betsy and the bicycle in tow, walked in the opposite direction to Max and Beyoncé, round the edge of Eye-Spy Wood and towards the ravine that separated it from the Forest of Fiends.

'How many monsters have we found now?' Grace asked Frank. 'I haven't been adding them up.'

Frank tapped the device on his wrist. 'Well, we got n-nineteen out of Eye-Spy Wood alone – a Tickle Monster, two Twitter Trolls, a Chatterbox Brownie, three Leprechauns, two Poo Shufflers, two Tripper Uppers, a Homework

Taker, a gang of five Parent Punishers, a Tree Hugger and, last but not least, a Biscuit Monster called E-Eddy. So, those added to the other eleven, m-means that thirty out of forty-three have been captured. No Johnny Big-Hands, though. Still got him to look forward to.'

'We should just leave the others,' said Mr Harris. 'I don't suppose anyone will notice.'

'I think Colonel Hardy might!' Grace said. As she spoke, something caught her eye, just off the path, inside the first line of trees at the edge of Eye-Spy Wood. A flash of rainbow colours. 'Won't be a minute!' she said, darting off, Kenny dangling from her shoulder.

'Doughnut Lady! Get back here!' cried Mr Harris behind her. 'You will not purposely delay my trip. This is a cyclops reunion of the greatest importance – because I am involved in it . . .'

'I think you'd better come here,' Grace called back.

'Oh no,' the cyclops said, shaking his head.

'I am not leaving this path to look at a wildflower or an interestingly shaped twig. Shrimp Boy! Do not listen to her, come back here!'

'I think it's i-important, Mr Harris, to look at what she's found,' called Frank as he scurried towards Grace.

Moaning and huffing, the cyclops stomped over to where Grace and Frank were standing.

'You called me over because you've found an abandoned wellington boot in a garish colour,' he said disbelievingly. 'Have I been pranked? Honestly, I have had it up to here with . . .' Mr Harris raised one hand above his head and began to sniff the air intently. 'Hang on.' He sniffed more, gradually getting closer to the rainbow-coloured welly Grace was holding up. 'Rose petals, horse poo, just a whiff of sherbet . . . that's NEVILLE'S BOOT!'

'Exactly,' said Grace. 'Look, there's an abandoned tent here too. He must have camped here at some point.'

'How in the name of Godzilla did that leathery old reptile survive?' boomed Mr Harris.

The screen on Grace's phone burst into life, interrupting the cyclops's rant.

Kenny shot forward and hit the 'answer' button. Danni's face appeared, a smear of flour across one cheek.

'Danni! Neville's alive!' cried Grace before her sister could say anything.

'That's what I was calling to tell you!' said Danni hurriedly. 'I've checked the Monster Scanner. He's in Monster World, Grace!'

'Oh, we know,' Grace replied, turning the video phone's camera towards the shabby tent and the wellington boot. 'We've literally just found his old hideout.'

'You must be careful,' said Danni. 'He could be anywhere. There wasn't a specific location on the Monster Scanner. I'll ask Mum or Dad to double-check for me when they're back, in case I missed something.'

'Mum and Dad!' cried Grace. 'Are they okay?'

'They're fine. On their way back now with another nine monsters captured,' Danni replied. 'Would you believe it, I caught two here, in the bakery? A Snack Snaffler and a Pie Pincher were fighting over a cherry and almond muffin. They were actually inside the glass display case, behind the counter. It was lucky there were no customers.'

Grace breathed a sigh of relief to hear that her parents were safe. Then she asked, 'What did you do about the monsters in the bakery?'

While her older sister could wield a tub of baking powder as well as any member of the Hunter family, she was much more at home being an expert cake-maker.

Danni grinned. 'Tore the muffin in half and told them to help themselves. They exploded at almost exactly the same time. Anyway, that's not important. What are you going to do about Neville?'

Grace took a deep breath. 'We're going to find him and destroy him. Again,' she said.

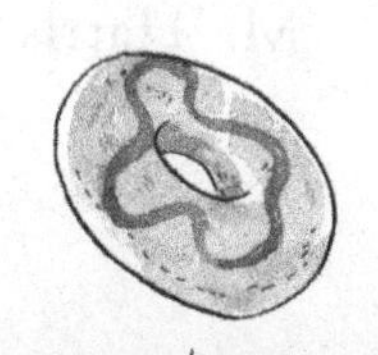

CHAPTER NINETEEN

Red Rock Ravine

'Knowing Neville's here somewhere is making me a little n-nervous,' Frank said as they walked away from Eye-Spy Wood. 'Hopefully, Dad might find out what's going on when he gets to the prison.'

'Man up, Shrimp Boy,' snapped Mr Harris. 'I have a secret cave and a mother to find as quickly as possible, and no inconveniently regenerated leathery lizard is going to get in my way.'

'We can't ignore the fact that he's here!' said Grace. On her shoulder, Kenny nodded vigorously.

Mr Harris stared at the Key Catcher. 'That

stick insect needs to keep its opinions to itself. And, Doughnut Lady, I didn't say I was going to ignore Neville. I'm just putting him on hold. I will carry out my important family business first. And when that's done, I will once again obliterate that scabby old scoundrel from the face of the earth. Frankly, I'm extremely annoyed it didn't work the first time. You obviously did something wrong when we found him in the Prime Minister's office.' He stopped dead in his tracks. 'Right, who's going first?'

Grace looked at what Mr Harris was gesturing to. They had reached a rickety fence at the edge of the deepest ravine Grace had ever seen. The rock face was a dark, earthy red and the drop was so deep, she couldn't see the bottom.

'Oh my g-goblins,' said Frank. 'R-Red Rock Ravine.'

On Grace's shoulder, Kenny crossed his arms and shook his head. The only good

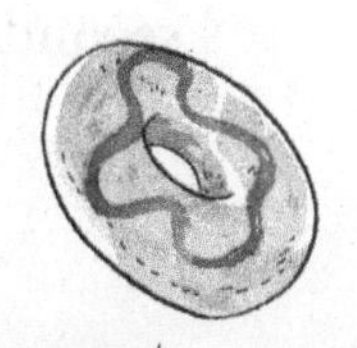

thing that Grace could see was that the distance to the other side – a thick wall of dark, looming trees – was reasonably short.

'How on earth are we meant to get across that?' asked Grace. 'There's no bridge.'

The cyclops rolled his eye in exasperation. 'The zip wire is perfectly safe.'

'Zip wire?' said Grace, her eyes widening as she caught sight of a flimsy wire that stretched across the ravine, attached to a tree on either side. 'That zip wire?' Her tone was disbelieving. 'We can't! It's too dangerous.'

Mr Harris was stony-faced. 'Well, stay here then. I didn't want you to muscle in on my private mission anyway.' Ignoring a set of rubber wrist loops attached to the zip wire, he shoved Betsy under one of his sizeable arms, balanced the bike precariously on the wire and hopped onto it, and shot off at about one hundred miles an hour.

He reached the other side in a matter of seconds.

'All yours!' he yelled, jumping off the bike and thrusting the unused wrist loops back along the wire towards them. Then he stomped off into the trees.

'You've got to be kidding,' said Grace, catching one of the rubber loops.

Kenny covered his eyes and dive-bombed into her pocket.

'I c-can't do this,' said Frank, his big eyes wide with terror.

'Mr Harris has just done it with a huge bike and a donkey. We can do this, Frank. Shall we go together? I'm not sure I want to do it on my own,' said Grace.

'O-Okay,' stammered Frank, beads of sweat popping out on his forehead under his blond curls.

Grace pulled the rubber loops towards Frank, who put his fork in his pocket, pushed his shaking hands through the loops and held on tight. The loops were big enough for Grace's hands to fit through too. Together, they edged closer towards the edge of the ravine.

'It's now or never.' Grace gulped.

'I'm n-not sure I . . . AAAARGH!' Frank screamed as they pushed off the side of the ravine and hurtled towards the trees on the other side.

They landed with a thud. Grace and Frank disentangled their hands from the loops as quickly as possible and crawled away from the edge.

'Frank? Are you okay?' Grace asked breathlessly. 'Kenny?'

Frank nodded, too shocked to speak, and Kenny raised a single shaky thumb.

'I hope there's another way back,' Grace muttered.

A scrawled, wonky sign by a path leading into the forest read, *Welcome to the Forest of Fiends. Enjoy your trip! It could be your last . . .*

They got unsteadily to their feet and made their way into the trees. It didn't take them long to find Mr Harris, casually cycling along, Betsy trudging behind him.

'You didn't plunge to your death, then?' he said.

'No, you must be delighted to see that we survived. And now we're ready to help you find your mum and track down Neville,' said Grace sarcastically.

'Slow me down, you mean,' said Mr Harris. Suddenly, he stopped. 'Ooh! Look!' He leaned down and plucked a perfectly round, bright red creature wearing a small black and white jumpsuit from the long grass at the side of the path. 'A Gobstopper Grub!' he cried in delight. 'Yum!'

Before Grace could stop him, he dropped it into his mouth.

'Mr Harris!' shouted Grace. 'You can't eat the prisoners! Spit him out!'

Mr Harris shook his head and swallowed loudly. 'You gave away my cake, I've eaten a prisoner. Fair's fair. I was snacky and he was delicious. Strawberry flavour! Undertones of basil too.'

'Unbelievable,' she said. Then she turned to Frank. 'That monster was very small to have made it such a long way from the prison.'

'Perhaps he came across with the last prisoner on the list?' Frank replied.

'That would be handy,' said Grace. 'Capture all the prisoners, find Gertrudetta, then head back to the bakery for a well-earned doughnut. But hang on, isn't the last prisoner on the list –'

Mr Harris's bicycle came to another sudden halt. Betsy, then Grace, then Frank bumped into the back of Mr Harris, who was looking upwards at something. Something big. Something that was blocking their path.

'Who's been eating my Gobstopper Grubs?' it bellowed, its enormous hands balled into fists at its sides.

'Number one,' murmured Frank, grabbing Grace's elbow. 'Johnny Big-Hands. Non-compliant Giant.'

CHAPTER TWENTY

Johnny Big-Hands

'He ate it!' spluttered Mr Harris, pointing at Frank.

The giant stared at the cyclops, then at Frank. 'He's too small. It wouldn't have fitted into his mouth.' He looked confused. He narrowed his eyes. 'You're the only one big enough to have eaten it. YOU ATE MY SWEET!' The giant's thunderous voice echoed round the trees, making the leaves shiver.

Mr Harris whipped around frantically, searching for something or someone else he could blame. 'I didn't realise it was yours,' he blurted.

'Here, take this donkey. She'll be absolutely delicious.'

The giant scowled. 'I'm pescatarian,' he said.

'Take these children!' spluttered Mr Harris. He pointed at Frank. 'I call this one Shrimp Boy – he's practically a fish. And this other one – well, I've eaten her myself in the past and, actually, she tastes like sweetened shortcrust pastry so she'll go well with Shrimp Boy.'

'Mr Harris!' said Grace through gritted teeth. 'We might need to think of a way out of this situation, rather than you offering us up as lunch.'

Johnny Big-Hands fixed his eyes onto Mr Harris, then Grace, then Frank, his nostrils flared, his knuckles white. All of a sudden, his shoulders slumped. 'I don't want to eat any of you! I just want to go back to the prison. Escaping seemed like a good idea when that lady said I should run away with the others. The happiness hub sounded so fun and exciting. But I don't think it was a good idea. I'm so tired.' He flopped down cross-legged on the path and sank his head into his enormous hands.

Grace raised her eyebrows. 'If you don't mind me asking,' she said, 'who said you should run away?'

'The lady who comes to the prison. I'm not supposed to talk about it, though. It's all a big secret,' said Johnny Big-Hands, looking uncomfortable.

'I understand,' said Grace. 'But there's a chance that this lady has done something really bad, so anything you can tell us would be a huge help. For example, what does she look like? Is she very small?'

The giant shook his head. 'No.'

Frank shot Grace a look of confusion. 'Oh, right. So she's not small, like Dr Darvill, for instance?'

'No, she's much bigger than Dr Darvill. And much less scary,' said the giant, folding his arms round himself protectively.

'Strange,' whispered Frank to Grace. 'Maybe it's not Dr Darvill who helped the prisoners escape?'

'Or she's working with someone else,' Grace hissed back.

'Hang on!' cried Mr Harris. 'Was she small and neat and bossy? Was she called Patricia? I knew it would be that rule-keeping, boring, old bag from Monster World Authorities Headquarters . . .'

But Johnny Big-Hands shook his head vigorously.

'But is she a troll?' Mr Harris demanded. 'Cheap creatures, untrustworthy.'

'No!' boomed Johnny Big-Hands. 'She's like you. A cyclops!'

Grace gasped. 'Beyoncé?' she mouthed to Frank, her eyes wide.

Mr Harris scowled. 'I think you're mistaken.'

'I don't care! I want to go back to the prison now,' Johnny Big-Hands whined. 'I like my little grey room, and my comfy bed, and the yummy

jelly for dessert, and the lessons, and the board games. I was learning chess!' He burst into a fit of noisy, snotty tears.

'Oh my goodness, don't cry,' said Grace. 'We can help you get back. Would you like us to call someone?'

The giant nodded. 'Yes, please. I knew I shouldn't have run away. I like the prison. I pretended to like bone-crushing just to get in there. I don't like bone-crushing at all!' He began to sob again.

'Good grief,' muttered Mr Harris. 'What an absolute waste of a giant.'

Grace elbowed him in the side. 'Please don't worry. Frank is going to call someone to come and get you now. You'll be back in no time.'

'The signal is weak,' said Frank. 'But there's probably enough to send a message.' He tapped at his wrist.

'Right, well, I'm glad that's all sorted,' said Mr Harris. 'I'm going to get on with my important mission now. I have a secret cave to find.'

'All the secret caves are up there,' said the giant, waving his gigantic hand behind him. 'Take the first left into the forest. I found them earlier, but that's when I started to think I wanted to be back in my lovely soft bed.' He blew his nose on the sleeve of his jumpsuit.

As Mr Harris strode away, Grace called after

him. 'Mr Harris, wait! It won't be long until help arrives. We can come with you after that.'

'I've got a reply! Dad says they're sending a helicopter. They should only be a few minutes,' said Frank.

'A few minutes I haven't got, Shrimp Boy,' said Mr Harris, continuing to walk away.

'I won't run away!' said Johnny. 'I promise to stay here until they collect me. I want to go back. Hopefully, they'll extend my sentence. I could say I ate you, like *he* suggested.' He pointed at Mr Harris, who was smiling smugly.

'Oh, no, don't do that,' said Grace. 'We can make sure they extend your sentence if that's what you really want.'

Johnny clapped his hands and nodded enthusiastically. 'Go after that grumpy cyclops. I'll stay here. I've never been in a helicopter before!'

Kenny jumped up and down on Grace's shoulder, pointing to himself and then the giant.

He leapt down from Grace's shoulder, scampered up Johnny Big-Hands' leg and coiled himself round his wrists, stretching, getting longer and longer.

Grace frowned. 'Okay, but Kenny, go with him and stay with Max until we get back. I don't want you getting lost.'

Kenny peeled one arm away and saluted like an army major.

'I'm cuffed!' said the giant delightedly. 'Can't go anywhere now, can I? We'll just wait here and it'll be prison sweet prison in no time!'

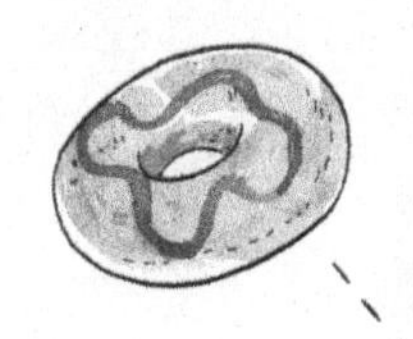

CHAPTER TWENTY-ONE

The Sign

Grace and Frank dashed off to catch up with Mr Harris, who was now quite far ahead. Luckily, they could hear the clip-clop of Betsy's hooves and the occasional *hee-haw* in the distance, so they knew they were on the right track.

'The cyclops must be Beyoncé!' said Frank, worry etched onto his face.

'Well, it seems that way,' Grace replied. 'Her job at the Monster World Authorities could be a front. She could even be working with Dr Darvill. Perhaps that's why she was so quick to tell us how reliable Dr Darvill is – to throw us off the scent!'

'Dad's with them b-both,' said Frank, gripping his fork tightly, his knuckles white. 'What if he's in d-danger?'

'Have you sent him a message?' asked Grace.

Frank nodded. 'Just now. But the signal is t-terrible again. It's fine one minute and not the n-next.'

'We could be wrong,' said Grace. 'It might not be either of them.'

'Maybe,' said Frank. 'But I d-doubt there are many cyclopes that visit the p-prison. What will Mr H-Harris do? He's got a soft spot for her.'

'Let's not mention it for now,' Grace said, her voice low. 'Let's just help him find his mum. Hopefully, Max will have replied to your message by then and we might know a bit more about what's going on – you know, before we ruin Mr Harris's life. Mr Harris, we're back!'

'Oh good,' said the cyclops flatly. 'I already feel like I've slowed down and become less efficient. You're such a terrible hindrance.'

Grace ignored him. 'So, do we know anything about the secret cave we're looking for?'

'I'll know it when I see it,' the cyclops replied. 'My mother has always been very particular about her homes having kerb appeal.'

'But they're secret caves . . .' said Grace. 'Doesn't that mean they'll be hidden away and difficult to find?'

Mr Harris took a deep breath. 'No, Doughnut Lady, it does not. We are in Monster World. *Secret Cave* could simply be the name of the building, or the cul-de-sac it's in. It doesn't necessarily mean it's actually a secret. And if it is, I'll still find it.'

'Monster World makes no sense,' Grace said.

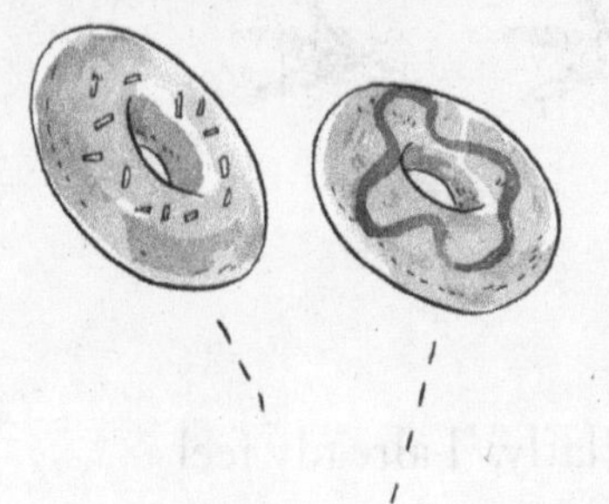

As they trudged on, the rocks and boulders grew bigger and flatter. Grace began to notice doors and windows in some of them, cleverly crafted from wood and stone, or painted green and brown to camouflage with their surroundings.

'These are houses!' she said.

Mr Harris took his hands off the handlebars and slow-clapped as he continued to pedal. 'Was it the garages that gave it away, or the signs with the house names?' he asked sarcastically.

'Garages? House names?' Grace said, twisting round to look more carefully.

'There,' said Frank pointing to a rickety wooden sign, well hidden among leaves.

'Creepy-Crawly Cottage,' read Grace. 'Sounds lovely. Oh look, another one – and you're right, Mr Harris, this one has a garage!'

'Sshhh!' hissed the cyclops. 'This is the Forest

of Fiends, Doughnut Lady. *Fiends* live here! Look, that house over there has claw marks all over it, and it's called Werewolf Towers. Werewolves are grouchy and bitey. Let's not draw attention to ourselves by getting excited over something as boring as a garage.'

'Sorry,' said Grace. 'But this garage is not boring. It has what looks like a camel in it. Its head is poking out of the window!'

'Read the sign, thicko! That's not a camel,' said Mr Harris, pedalling faster to get away.

'Alpaca Apartments and Ranch,' Frank read out loud.

Grace tutted. 'I was close enough. Do I even want to ask why there are alpacas in Monster World?'

Frank shook his head vigorously.

They passed more buildings and more garages. One had most of a yacht poking out of it; another contained a bouncy castle covered in jumping, squealing, tiny monsters.

Grace was so distracted by the peculiar location, she almost didn't see the unlit neon sign that had fallen over at the point where the path split into different directions.

'Oh! Mr Harris! I think I've found it!' she called.

The cyclops stopped pedalling. He hauled himself off his bicycle, and dumped it at the side of the path, patted Betsy's head and stomped towards Grace and Frank.

'*Residential*,' he read from the left-side of a flashing digital sign that was still standing. Then he read the other side. '*Path to imminent danger*. Wow, Doughnut Lady, your memory is worse than I thought it was. We are searching for *secret caves*.' He spoke slowly and simply, as though he was talking to a small and difficult child.

'Not those ones,' Grace snapped. 'This one on the ground. It's fallen over.'

Mr Harris cast his eye downwards to the fallen sign. It lay on the ground, not far from another sign which appeared to, very helpfully, point in the direction of *Imminent Danger*.

'*Secret Caves*,' he read. 'Oh, how clever! No one looks at a sign that's lying in the grass, do they? How brilliantly secretive.'

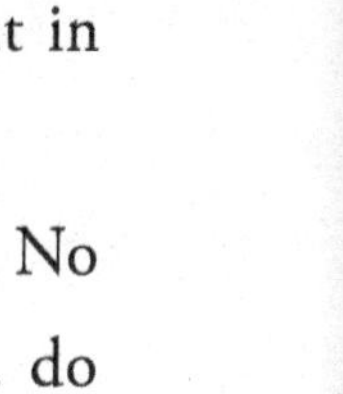

'*I* looked,' Grace muttered.

'And it's *neon*,' added Frank.

Mr Harris barged past Grace and Frank and began to push branches and bushes aside. 'A gate!' he cried. Then he lowered his voice. 'Oh – and a pesky troll. Would you believe it? Why do they take these jobs when the risk of being eaten is so high? Hold on.'

Mr Harris disappeared into the trees. A few seconds later, there was a loud gulp.

'I'm through!' he announced. 'Are you slow-coaches coming?'

CHAPTER TWENTY-TWO

The Secret Cave

Behind the gate was a neat courtyard, lined with raised vegetable beds sprouting all sorts of leafy greens and herbs. In the middle of the beds was a large stone water feature – a fish with water spraying out of its mouth into a pond below. The water swished and swashed so calmly, Grace felt that, if she closed her eyes, she could almost mistake it for the sound of the sea.

On the far side of the courtyard loomed a vast rock face of slate grey with a tall, rounded opening at the bottom. Two beautiful rose bushes, bursting with red-petalled flowers, sat on either side of the entrance, along with a rather strangely placed pair of silver roller skates. The area was edged with giant trees which formed a thick wall around it.

'It's really beautiful here,' said Grace.

'It has my mother written all over it,' said Mr Harris matter-of-factly. 'Vegetables, flowers, water. Throw in a maths equation and a roller disco, and it's everything she likes all in one place.'

'Are you going to knock?' asked Grace. 'Do you want us to come with you?'

'To get in the way of a private family reunion? No, thank you,' said Mr Harris. 'You can wait for me out here. I won't be more than a few hours.'

'A f-few hours?' asked Frank. 'What are we going to do?'

'Yes, Shrimp Boy, a few hours. We have more than a few decades to catch up on,' Mr Harris replied. 'What you do to pass the time is not *my* problem. I said you shouldn't have come.'

'Always so grateful for help and support!' said

Grace chirpily. 'Now, Mr Harris, don't be cross at me for suggesting this, but do you think you should mention Neville to your mum? In case she's heard from him? Or in case she's in danger?'

'Danger?' Mr Harris laughed. 'Not a chance. He's her father and they're annoyingly close. She's the only other being that stinky old stoat will give the time of day to.'

'Well then, it's definitely worth mentioning him to her. What if he's made contact with her?' said Grace.

'That would be second on his list. Destroying *me* would be priority number one for Neville the Devil,' said Mr Harris, his teeth gritted. 'You must both remember how much he hates me – his more handsome, more important, more successful, way more buff grandson.'

Grace snorted with laughter but, on seeing the cyclops's glare, coughed loudly in an attempt to cover up her amusement.

Mr Harris continued to glare, then stamped off towards the door.

'Perhaps you should've got her a present?' said Grace as she and Frank hurried alongside the cyclops.

'Well, I could have shared my cake with her, but you recklessly gave it away. I'll tell her there's a bike out there by the path for her,' he said. He paused. 'She's not having my donkey.'

The cavernous hole in the slate opened out into a smart porch area. From outside, Grace could see a wooden door set into the inner wall. Tinkling wind chimes and colourful lanterns hung from the stone ceiling. A pile of firewood was tucked into the corner of the porch, next to a muddy pair of boots, which sat on a rubber mat.

'Why are you still following me?' Mr Harris said. 'Go and sniff the herbs or something. Chuck a penny into that fishy fountain.'

'Charming,' said Grace. 'Well, good luck, Mr Harris. I hope the reunion goes well. Please don't take too long, though, as we really do need to get back to the prison. You can always come back here afterwards.'

Frank nodded. 'Good luck, Mr Harris.'

'Oh, do stop your sentimental nonsense,' Mr Harris said, grimacing as he stepped inside the porch. 'We cyclopes are factual, purposeful creatures. My mother and I will reunite in a formal manner, we will have a cup of some sort of disgusting herbal tea that she likes, we will exchange stories – not the one about her father exploding – and I will leave. There will be no crying, no hugging, and no vomit-inducing show of unnecessary emotions. Thank you.'

Just as Mr Harris finished speaking, the wooden door flew open. There was a flurry of movement as something launched itself at him, enveloping him in a bear hug, planting loud kisses all over his cheeks.

'STEVIE! My beautiful boy! You came! How I've missed you!' cried a cyclops with long red hair and a flowery apron. Huge tears dripped from her eye onto the floor. 'I could sense you were here, then I heard your voice!' she continued through sobs of joy. 'And you *are* here! Oh, look at you, Stevie, all grown-up and handsome. We have so much catching up to do! Come in! Let me get you a mint tea!'

CHAPTER TWENTY-THREE

He's Back

As the door slammed behind them, Grace said, 'I thought he said there would be no hugging or crying?'

Frank giggled. 'She calls him S-Stevie! He'd eat us if we called him that.'

'At least she was pleased to see him. She mustn't know he exploded her dad.' Grace laughed, once again taking in the homely porch. It was easier to have a good look around without a cyclops reunion taking place. Suddenly, her heart skipped a beat.

'Frank, look.' She gestured to the rubber mat with the muddy boots on it. Stuffed behind them, lying on its side, was a single wellington boot. It was rainbow-coloured.

Frank's eyes were wide. 'And look what's up there too.' He pointed above the wooden door. There was a small hand-carved sign. It read *The Hub*. In between the two words was a carving of a sun with a happy face, lines of light stretching out from it.

'The happiness hub,' Grace whispered. 'Neville is here, Frank. We thought Johnny Big-Hands was talking about Beyoncé. He wasn't. He was talking about Gertrudetta!'

'I need to call D-Dad,' said Frank.

Grace took out the video phone. 'Still no signal. What do we do? Do you have any on your device?'

Frank shook his head. He lifted his wrist higher into the air, the video phone in his other hand, and walked quietly round the courtyard, checking every few seconds to see if the signal on either had improved.

'How about trying over there?' Grace suggested, pointing to the far edge of the clearing, where a satellite dish sat above a window.

Frank hurried towards it, holding his arms out in front of him. When he reached the window, he stopped dead.

'Oh my goblins. Grace, c-come over here.' His voice was low.

At first glance, the space appeared to be a bedroom. There was a wooden bed in one corner with a woollen blanket on top of it, folded neatly. A wardrobe stood against the far wall with a chest of drawers pushed up to its side. There was a high-backed chair with a single crutch leaning against it and a shaggy rug on the floor. And a silver laptop sat on a small desk, a closed notebook beside it.

But one of the walls was more unusual.

Masses of photographs and sticky notes covered every

inch of it. There were pictures of the monsters who had escaped from Monster World Prison, with their names, strengths and weaknesses marked next to them. Grace immediately noticed that there was a red cross scrawled across the photo of Brandy McNap, the Sleep Stealer Frank had carried through Monster World. Next to it, in capital letters, tidy handwriting said COMPLETELY USELESS. She recognised a photo of Bruce Goblin, who they had found snared by the Ankle Grabber near Eye-Spy Wood. Next to him was a note that said DEVIOUS. She could see photos of the Chatterbox Brownie, Dirk the Destroyer, even Johnny Big-Hands (his note said EXCELLENT STRENGTH, BUT A COMPLETE WET BLANKET).

On another wall, adjacent to the monsters' mugshots were grainy photos of every member of the Hunter family – and Mr Harris. Each had a target number underneath them. Mr Harris was number one. Grace was number two.

'Well, Neville's been busy,' said Grace.

Frank held up the video phone. 'It's ringing!'

'Grace, Frank!' said Danni, as her face filled the tiny screen.

Eamon's face pushed in next to Danni's.

'Where are you now?'

'We're at Gertrudetta's,' said Grace. 'Dad, Neville's alive. For sure. This is a trap! And Mr Harris is inside!'

'We've just found out the same thing, from Colonel Hardy. She spoke to Dr Darvill. Gertrudetta has been teaching at the prison,' said Eamon. 'While she was there, she managed to track down the prisoners who used to follow Neville when he was trying to take over our world, plus others. She told them that Neville was alive and convinced them to escape and follow him again. She's extremely close to her father and would do anything for him . . . even lure her own son to her cave so Neville could finish off what he tried to do at 10 Downing Street. You and Frank need to leave, Grace. Now. You're in danger!'

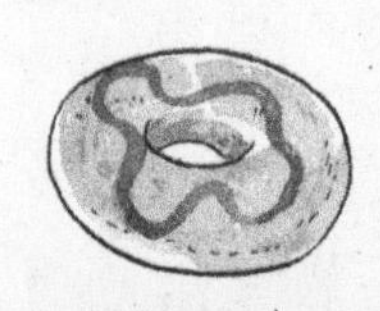

CHAPTER TWENTY-FOUR

Neville

As Frank hung up, Grace turned to him. 'I can't leave Mr Harris,' she said. 'You can go, Frank, but I can't. I'm really sorry.'

'I'm n-not going anywhere,' Frank replied. 'We've defeated Neville once, Grace, and we can do it again.'

Grace threw herself at Frank and hugged him tightly.

'Bet I wouldn't have said that a few weeks ago,' said Frank, smiling shyly.

'You're so different now, Frank – so brave!' said Grace. 'Which is just as well, seeing as we're about to walk into a cave containing three cyclopes.'

Frank held his fork out in front of him. 'I'm r-ready.'

'Have you got plenty of baking powder?' asked Grace, patting down her pockets for her stash of the deadly, monster-destroying powder.

'In every pocket,' said Frank, lifting one pot out of his trouser pocket. 'So, what will we do once we get inside?'

'We have to take him down straight away. Throw everything we've got at him,' said Grace. 'Let's go to the front door and hope Gertrudetta was forgetful enough to leave it unlocked.'

They tiptoed to the porch area with the lanterns and wind chimes, the logs and the worrying footwear. Grace crept towards the front door and rested her hand lightly on the handle. The moment she touched it, it was wrenched out of her hand and the door flew open.

'Don't whisper out here, children!' Neville said brightly, his oval, snake-like eye glistening with excitement. In one hand he gripped a metal crutch, but he still looked strong and menacing. 'Come in!'

Grace thrust her hand into her pocket and grabbed a pot of baking powder. But as soon as she lifted it out, it shot towards Neville as though it was pulled by a magnet. He caught it neatly in his black-clawed hand.

'Thank you,' he said. Like lightning, he did exactly the same to Frank's precious tub. 'I think it's best that you empty your pockets and leave your bag out here in the porch. We don't want any accidents, do we?'

Grace scowled. 'It wouldn't be an accident,' she muttered, shrugging her rucksack off her shoulders and letting it land with a thud on the floor beside her. She took another pot of baking powder out of her trouser pocket and placed it sulkily on the floor, but made no attempt to

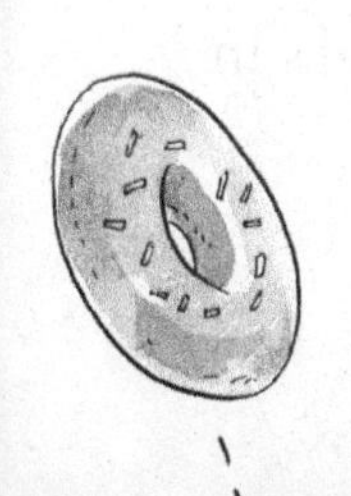

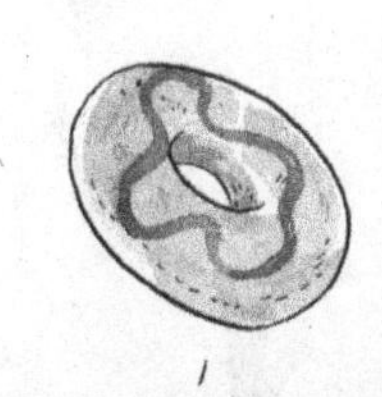

remove the small, resealable plastic bag of baking powder from the other pocket, where she had put it for emergencies just like this one.

Frank placed four tubs of baking powder onto the ground by his feet. Grace was sure he also had a secret sachet hidden somewhere.

'And the fork, the phone and your watch, or whatever it is,' Neville added, eying Frank's wrist suspiciously.

'Not my f-fork,' Frank pleaded.

Neville pointed at it, then drew his hand downwards. The fork flew out of Frank's grasp and clattered to the floor.

'Now, get inside,' Neville hissed.

As they entered the hallway, Neville shut and locked the door behind them. 'Go straight through to the kitchen at the back,' he snapped. 'Your friend's in there too.'

Grace walked to the far end of the hall, Frank close behind her, the hand that would usually be gripping his fork curled tightly into a fist. She pushed open the aged, wooden door.

Mr Harris sat at a large oak table in the middle of the room, an open fire crackling behind him. He looked absolutely furious. Gertrudetta was stirring something on the hob behind him, chattering happily. There were shelves holding hundreds of different coloured jars and bottles above the stove.

'. . . And I said that anyone can do maths, it's easy as pi! Did you get the joke, Stevie? Easy as pie . . . but I meant pi . . . as in maths!' Gertrudetta cried, turning round as the door opened. 'Oh, Stevie's friends! How lovely! Mint tea?' She pushed her long red hair behind one of her green ears.

'They don't want mint tea!' barked Mr Harris. 'They're about to die! At least give them some milk and a biscuit.'

Gertrudetta giggled. 'You do make me laugh, Stevie, but that's very dark. Of course they're not going to die. You're here to talk through why you felt it necessary to blow up your Grandpops, and to apologise properly. That's all. Isn't that right, Papa?' She looked at Neville with a big, hopeful eye.

'Exactly, Gerty,' Neville said soothingly. 'We're just going to chat about why they felt they could blast someone as important and powerful as me into a billion tiny pieces.'

'See?' said Gertrudetta happily.

'How can someone so good at maths be so unbelievably stupid?' mumbled Mr Harris, jerking his body in the chair, as though he couldn't get up. 'If we're only here to talk, why are my arms and legs bound by invisible string so I can't move them?'

'You tried to punch your Grandpops the moment you saw him, darling,' said Gertrudetta, frowning. 'It's for his own protection, while he recovers to full strength. You could have set him back weeks if you'd hit him.'

'You punch him, Shrimp Boy!' Mr Harris yelled suddenly. 'You could set him back a second or two! Go on, Doughnut Lady, right-hook the old worm! Take him down with your feeble excuses for arms!'

'Enough!' shouted Neville sharply. His voice echoed round the room so loudly that Gertrudetta turned from the stove, her face anxious.

'Let's not bother talking. Let's just get to the good bit. The bit I've been waiting for every minute of every hour of every day while my body rebuilt itself. I have pictured this moment over and over again. And now it's time.'

A vein in Neville's neck flexed. His eye was bulging with excitement.

'Time to hug and make up?' asked Gertrudetta.

'Mother!' said Mr Harris in exasperation. 'Does he look like a hugger to you?'

'He hugs me sometimes,' she said.

'While he convinces you to bust some monsters out of prison?' said Mr Harris, rolling his eye.

'That was for the greater good!' she cried. 'It was to help them find themselves again. And besides, Papa said that it wouldn't be a problem once he was in charge. He was going to explain the whole thing to the Monster World Authorities!'

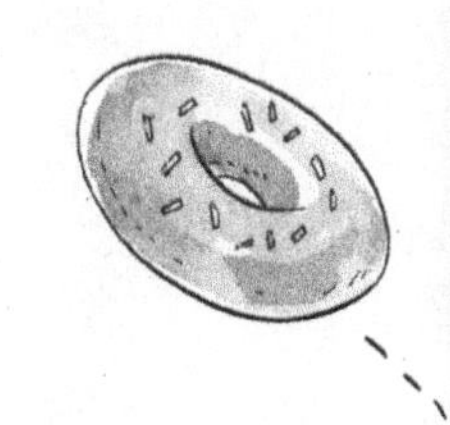

'After he'd burnt their offices down and eaten all their Document Devils?' Mr Harris enquired.

'No! He wouldn't do that . . . would you, Papa?' said Gertrudetta pleadingly.

'Of course not, little Gerty,' said Neville. He smiled, and his razor-sharp teeth glistened. 'Document Devils taste of metal.'

Gertrudetta beamed back at him.

Mr Harris let out a growl of frustration and looked from Grace to Frank, then nodded towards his mum. 'She's got a doctorate in maths, for goodness' sake! She can multiply six hundred and twenty-two thousand, three hundred and ninety-seven by four hundred and fifty-one in her head, but she can't spot the festering fibber right under her nose!'

'Two hundred and eighty million, seven hundred and one thousand, and forty-seven,' whispered Gertrudetta.

Neville leapt forward.

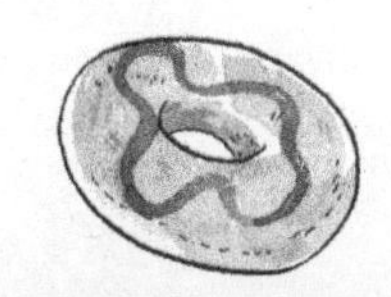

CHAPTER TWENTY-FIVE

Some Unexpected Help

Neville came to a stop an inch from Mr Harris's face.

'You tried to kill me,' Neville hissed.

'Clearly not hard enough,' Mr Harris muttered. 'I blame Doughnut Lady.'

'You ruined my plan, and you blew me up,' Neville continued. 'And now it's time for my revenge.'

'Papa, what do you mean?' said Gertrudetta, looking worried. 'Why don't you give Stevie some space?'

Neville ignored her, his eyes fixed on his

grandson. 'How are you feeling? Any last wishes?'

Mr Harris, stared back, unblinking. 'I wish you would step back a bit. I can't take much more of your breath. What did you have for breakfast? Cowpats on toast?'

Neville laughed, a long maniacal howl, his forked tongue whipping in and out of his open mouth. Abruptly, he stopped laughing and narrowed his oval eye. 'Very funny – you always were quite the clown. But if you have no last wishes, let's get on with this. I'll get rid of you first because you're so repulsively large and it'll zap my strength. Then I'll get to your little human friends. I can probably deal with them with just my index finger, they're so puny.'

'If you want to know why we did what we did, it was to stop you killing the Prime Minister and taking over our world with your army of monsters.' Grace stepped forward, conscious of keeping her hand as close

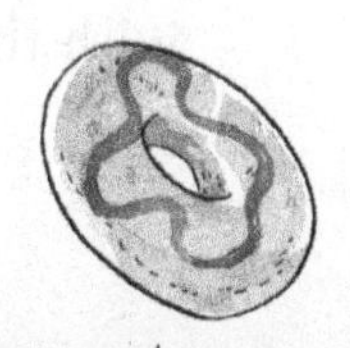

to the sachet of baking powder as she could without raising suspicion. 'And we'll do it again.'

Neville turned towards her, disgusted. 'You're unarmed. And this baboon can't move.' He jerked his head towards Mr Harris. 'You *can't* stop me.'

'Yes, we can!' yelled Grace, plunging her hand into her pocket and drawing out the plastic sachet.

Frank did the same just a millisecond later.

But before they'd had time to open them, both sachets shot towards Neville's outstretched hand.

'Well, that was a very stupid move,' jeered Neville, dumping the little plastic bags on the table in front of him. 'Gerty, cable-tie them now. I haven't the strength to keep them still without ties. Your great big goon of a son is zapping my energy. It's extremely annoying.'

Gertrudetta was noticeably flustered. 'But Papa, they're children. Perhaps we should just let them leave now? And maybe Stevie should go with them in case they get lost?'

'Now!' Neville boomed.

Gertrudetta shrank back and opened a drawer, pulling out some long plastic ties. She hurried over to Grace and Frank and gestured to the chairs round the table. After they had sat down, she secured their wrists to the backs of the chairs. Her big lilac-coloured eye had filled up with tears and she mouthed, 'Sorry,' to them as she shuffled back to her place by the stove.

'Come and sit here,' Neville barked at Gertrudetta, nodding to the last available kitchen chair. Obediently, she sat down. Quick as a flash, Neville cable-tied her hands in the same way as she had done Grace and Frank's.

'Papa!' she cried, her tears splashing down her cheek.

'You were always too sentimental, Gerty,' he snapped. 'I can't have you messing this up just because you feel sorry for those two ragamuffins.'

'You said you wouldn't hurt anyone!' she sobbed.

'Correct,' said Neville. 'I don't plan to hurt them. I plan to kill them. Since you're already an emotional wreck, I'll make it quick.'

'Scum,' breathed Mr Harris, his nostrils flaring in anger.

Neville raised one arm and crashed it down on the table in front of Mr Harris. The cyclops

jerked as though he had been physically hit, and his chair wobbled.

Frantically Grace scanned the kitchen, trying desperately to think of something she could do to retaliate and protect Mr Harris and Frank. With her hands tied, there was almost nothing she could do, so she worked on pushing them together and trying to ease them out of the stiff plastic cable-tie. Next to her, she could see Frank doing the same.

Her heart was banging so hard inside her chest, she was sure she could hear it thudding among Gertrudetta's sniffles and Neville's speech to Mr Harris about what a terrible disappointment he was. *Why didn't he want to assist a member of his own family in taking over Human World?* It wasn't until the kitchen door began to ease open that she realised the dull thumps she had heard had come from the front door, down the hall, not her heart.

She tried not to react and gazed at the floor to try and figure out who was pushing the door. She had to stop herself shouting aloud in delight when she saw a little Key Catcher squeezing through the tiny gap, pots of baking powder balanced in his hands.

CHAPTER TWENTY-SIX

Get Him!

She signalled to Frank with her eyes, and they watched as Kenny scampered soundlessly across the tiles. He stopped at the leg of Grace's chair and carefully put down the pots he was carrying. Then he scuttled up the chair's frame and along her arm to her wrist. Before he started to work on the cable-tie, he gave her arm a reassuring pat.

Grace could feel the Key Catcher working his spindly fingers through the loop and the mechanism that secured the tie in place. On the other side of the table, Neville was getting angrier. He banged his fist on the wooden surface, shouting about Mr Harris being a disgrace to the monster race.

Then, without warning, he twisted round towards Grace.

'Stop shuffling!' he demanded. 'You're trying to wriggle out of your restraints! Gerty, check they're on tight enough and then sit back down.'

With one flick of his black claw, the cable-tie securing Gertrudetta's hands flew into the air and she was able to pull herself up to standing. As she did, Grace felt her own cable-tie loosen and fall off her wrists. She braced herself to act fast.

Gertrudetta, sniffing sadly, walked behind Grace's chair. Grace tensed her legs, ready to drop to the floor and grab Kenny's baking powder. Her heart hammered against her ribs.

'The restraints are tight. I expect she's just uncomfortable,' Gertrudetta lied. She squeezed

Grace's shoulder and sat back down, allowing Neville to re-fasten her own hands.

Grace heard Frank breathe out in relief and saw, out of the corner of her eye, that Kenny had darted up his chair and was loosening his cable-tie as quickly as his gangly fingers would allow.

'Good. That means no interruptions to my grand finale,' Neville said, glaring at Mr Harris. 'Anything you'd like to say, disgraceful grandson of mine?'

Grace willed him to say something – anything – and buy Kenny a little more time.

Mr Harris cleared his throat. 'Yes, actually. As I can't see a way out of this unforeseen and very disappointing situation, I would like to say a few things.'

'Quickly,' said Neville through gritted, pointy teeth.

'I shall take as long as it requires,' Mr Harris replied. 'Mother, your father is a lying, murderous old goat and you didn't see through him. That's disappointing. Shrimp Boy, despite your pathetic size, your baby hair and your fork, you've got slightly braver. My doing, I expect, but anyway, good job. Doughnut Lady, I'd like to say that you're not that bad. You're bossy and annoying, yes. But I like my room at the bakery and I like the cakes, and I suppose, in some ways, you've been relatively useful. I hope this gnarly old snake-face doesn't kill you. If by some miracle he doesn't, tell Miss McDonald that I think she's a very fine cyclops, despite the cake-stealing.'

Mr Harris turned his head towards his grandfather and looked him up and down in disgust. 'The less said about you, the better.'

'Done?' barked Neville. 'Good. I was bored.'

As Neville raised both arms into the air, Frank's cable-tie dropped to the floor. Neville's chest was heaving, his shoulders shaking with tension, all his concentration focused on mustering his weakened power. Grace and Frank ducked and grabbed the baking powder from the floor.

Kenny soared through the air onto the table and scooped up one of the plastic sachets.

'NOW!' screeched Grace, just as Neville forced his arms down in a sweeping motion, giving a hollow, animal-like cry of effort.

At the same time, Grace and Frank threw themselves across the table, emptying both pots of

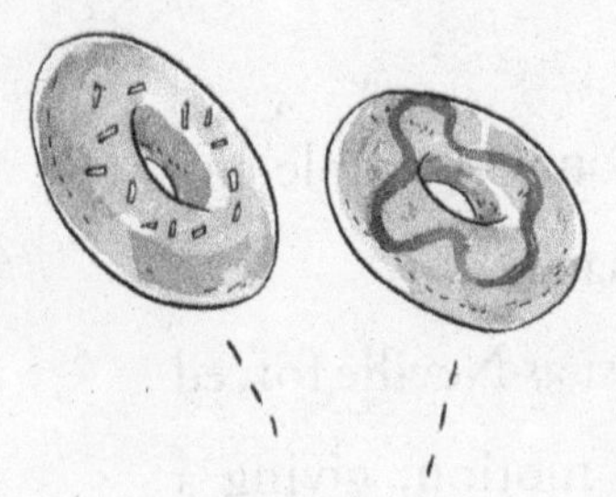

baking powder into Neville's eye. Kenny poured the sachet into his open mouth and all over his pointy, forked tongue.

With a guttural growl, Gertrudetta wrenched her arms free of the cable-tie, grabbed the last pouch of baking powder and jammed it into one of Neville's ears with an impressive karate chop and an angry screech.

'NO ONE hurts my Stevie!' she roared.

Neville howled, recoiling, shrinking, deflating like a balloon. He hissed and writhed, getting smaller and smaller, until he was no more than a mound of black dust on the tiled floor. Destroyed, again.

Without a word, Gertrudetta snatched a dustpan and brush, swept up Neville's remains, tipped half of the dust into the sink and the rest of it into the open fire at the back of the kitchen.

'Split the remains – fire and water. There's

no coming back from that,' she said under her breath.

Kenny jumped up and down on the table and punched the air in delight.

Grace felt her shoulders drop as she breathed out a huge sigh of relief. 'That was a bit too close for my liking,' she murmured, turning round. 'Mr Harris!'

The cyclops was slumped to one side and his eye was closed. As Grace rushed over to him, his chair creaked, then toppled over.

CHAPTER TWENTY-SEVEN

Wake Up, Please!

Grace and Frank dropped to their knees on either side of the cyclops, while Kenny stood on Mr Harris's face, pinching his cheeks.

'My baby!' screeched Gertrudetta, hurling herself to the floor and taking his arm and resting her fingers against his wrist.

'There's a pulse, but it's weak,' she said, a determined look in her eye despite the tears rolling down her face. 'I know what to do.' She jumped to her feet, seized a saucepan and darted towards the front door.

No more than thirty seconds later,

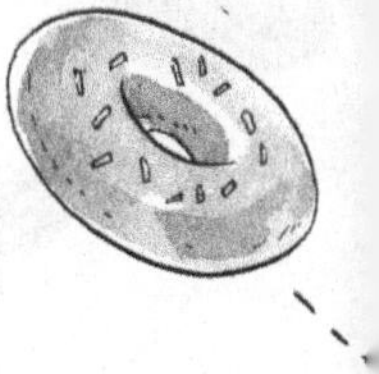

she returned, the pan overflowing with vibrant green and purple leaves and twisted spiral stalks and stems. Gertrudetta thrust the pan onto the stove and poured in some of her mint tea, along with splashes and pinches from some of the bottles and jars on the shelf above the hob. All the while she stirred, she chattered. She told tales about Mr Harris as a baby, stories of childhood events, how much she hated having lost contact with him, and how cross she was with herself for being so naïve about her father's plans.

When the pan was bubbling and frothing so much that its contents leaked over the edge and a cloud of green steam blasted from the top, Gertrudetta poured some of the liquid into a cup and knelt down by her unmoving son.

Together, Grace and Frank manoeuvred Mr Harris's huge head so it was tilted. Kenny prised open his lips so Gertrudetta could pour the liquid into his mouth.

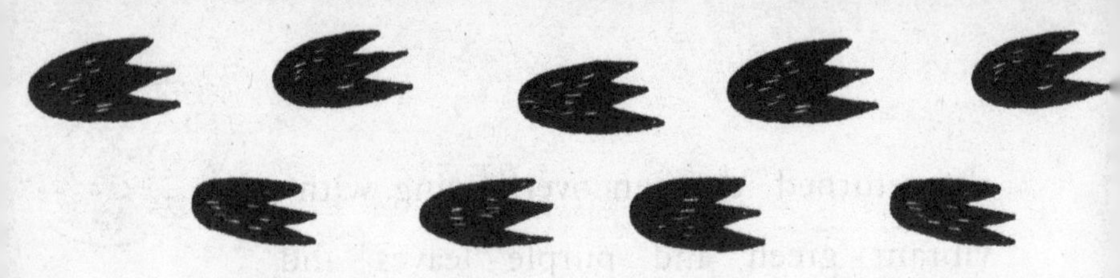

'Come on, Mr Harris,' Grace whispered, a tear rolling silently down her cheek.

The cyclops remained still.

Gertrudetta emptied the last few drops from the cup into his mouth and clasped his hands tightly in her own. 'I always loved him more than Papa, you know,' she said quietly. 'But they were both so strong-willed and so determined, they clashed all the time and argued. It was hard to be stuck in between them sometimes. It was worse when Stevie won the Monster World Board Game Championships. Papa saw that as an insult, a direct challenge. We drifted apart after that, as they couldn't stand to be around one another.'

Grace wiped her eyes on the back of her hand. 'I understand.'

'Papa could be scary, but he was always fiercely protective of me. I felt that I had to be loyal to

him because of that,' Gertrudetta continued, rubbing Mr Harris's hands over and over again. 'But Stevie was my pride and joy. He always had my heart. I thought we could all make up, you know. I thought if I could just get him here, then they could talk, work things out, you know? But I was so silly! So foolish! And look what I've done now.'

She collapsed into a convulsing heap of sobs.

'He was d-determined to find you,' ventured Frank.

Gertudetta looked up tearfully.

Grace nodded. 'He's been trying to track you down for a while. We know he wanted to make up,' she said kindly.

Gertudetta lowered her face to Mr Harris's chest and cried silently.

'I'm so sorry, Stevie,' she said, her voice muffled.

'For what?' came the weak but unmistakable sound of Mr Harris's voice. 'For letting my own grandfather try and kill me, or for making me drink what I'm sure will actually be the thing that finishes me off?'

'STEVIE!' yelled Gertrudetta at the same time as Grace and Frank screamed, 'MR HARRIS!'

Kenny danced a jig across the cyclops's shoulder.

'Keep it down,' moaned Mr Harris. 'I nearly died.'

Grace threw her arms round his neck. 'Never do that again,' she scolded, tears pouring down her cheeks.

'Be quicker with the baking powder next time, Doughnut Lady,' said Mr Harris quietly, patting her gently on the back.

CHAPTER TWENTY-EIGHT

Leave No One Behind

Mr Harris struggled to sit up, but eventually heaved himself off the floor. Grace knew he was weak and tired, even though he tried to cover it up. He collapsed into a chair and allowed Gertrudetta to bring him a cocktail of natural remedies she had prepared.

'This is for energy,' she announced, popping two big purple pills in front of him.

He swallowed them and winced. 'They taste of farts and broccoli,' he said.

'Yes! They are made of purple sprouting broccoli!' said Gertrudetta proudly. 'These are

for your joints, as you took quite a fall. These are for your head, in case it's achey. These are to help you get back on your feet. And put these ones in your pocket for later – they'll help you sleep.' She dropped an array of round and oval capsules in front of him. 'And here's some mint tea, which is good for everything.'

She placed a tray with four large cups of mint tea on the table. Kenny checked the heat of the liquid in one with a wispy finger before jumping in and doing breast-stroke to the other side.

'Oh! I'll make you sandwiches too. You need to get your strength back,' Gertrudetta said, bustling off to rummage in the larder.

Grace peered into Kenny's cup. 'Kenny, thank you so much for what you did. I can't bear to think what might have happened otherwise. Why did you come back when you were meant to be going to Monster World Prison with Johnny Big-Hands?'

Kenny pulled himself up onto the rim of the cup, his skinny legs dangling into the mint tea. He frowned and pointed to Grace and Frank.

'Were you worried about us?' asked Grace.

The Key Catcher nodded.

'You wanted to see the inside of a cyclops's house, more likely,' mumbled

Mr Harris. 'We'd have found a way out of that little predicament ourselves.'

'Mr Harris?' said Grace. 'Perhaps a thank you would be nice.'

The cyclops scowled. 'Thanks, Stick Face,' he said, so quietly it was barely audible. 'We would have been fine, though.'

Grace rolled her eyes. 'Well, now we know you're going to be okay, we should probably call Max and get back to the prison,' she said to Mr Harris. 'You can stay here with your mum until you're properly better.'

The cyclops baulked. 'I will do no such thing,' he said, spitting a mouthful of mint tea back into the cup with a look of distaste. 'I am leading this mission and I will be reporting back too!'

'Mr Harris, you can hardly stand. It's a long way. There's a zip wire too, for goodness' sake!' said Grace.

'We can take the suspension bridge with the electric walkway. Less zippy,' he said.

'There's a s-suspension bridge?' said Frank in disbelief. 'A suspension bridge we didn't use on the way here?'

'Yes, but it's a much longer route,' said Mr Harris. 'I've always found the zip wire to be much more efficient. Saves you a good five minutes.'

Frank groaned.

'Actually, once we've called Max and explained, they might send the helicopter,' Grace said excitedly.

'Oh no,' said Mr Harris, shaking his head. 'I did not just survive an attack by my evil grandfather, as well as that hideous concoction my mother gave me, to plummet to my death in a mechanical nightmare. Thank you very much.'

'Helicopters are perfectly safe,' said Grace. 'You'd be fine!'

'Nope. They're flown by the most reckless monsters,' he said. 'I'd rather crawl all the way to the prison with you, Shrimp Boy, the stick

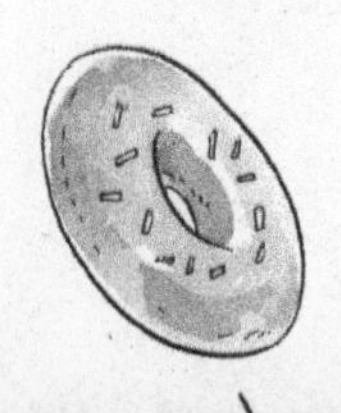

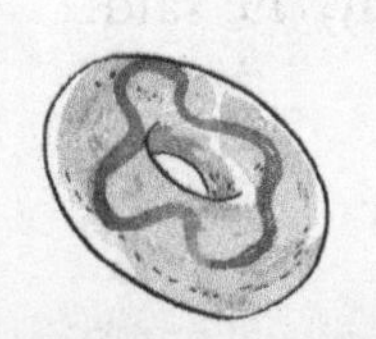

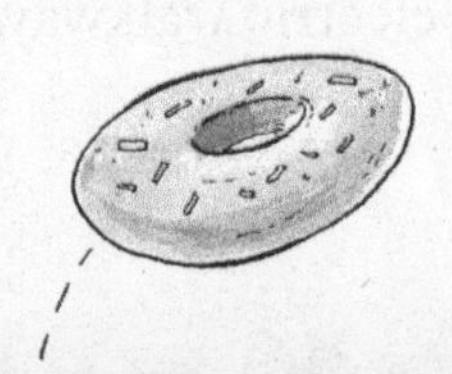

insect and Betsy on my back than set foot in one of those deathtraps. We shall be going on foot, Doughnut Lady. It's the least you can do for me after my ordeal.'

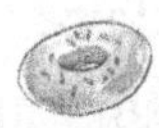

After they had eaten the towering sandwiches Gertrudetta made for them and after Mr Harris had swallowed his pills – promising to come back and see his mum for the proper catch-up they were due – they set off, collecting Betsy and Frank's treasured fork on their way. The strange bicycle was nowhere to be seen. While Mr Harris was outraged at the apparent theft, Grace was relieved that they had one less thing to drag along with them. She was concerned that they would be quite slow enough with a weakened, moany cyclops as part of their group.

They had barely got to the end of the track down to Gertrudetta's house before Mr Harris leaned heavily against a wall.

'I'm a little fatigued,' he said. 'I'll just rest here for a minute.'

'Mr Harris,' Grace said gently. 'Why don't you just go back to your mum's for a few days? We can handle this next bit. We'll tell them how brave you were, obviously.'

'No,' he replied firmly. 'I'm coming. I have unfinished business.'

'You can hardly walk,' Grace said.

'I'm fine!' he snapped. 'If only some pesky monster hadn't stolen my brilliant bike, we'd be at the prison by now.'

'No, we wouldn't,' said Grace patiently. 'Listen, Mr Harris, just –'

The cyclops's eye lit up as he clasped his hands. 'I don't need the bike!' he announced.

'Well, you need something. And resting at your mum's house, being looked after, would be the best thing –' Grace started.

Mr Harris brushed her out of the way and barged past with a sudden burst of energy. 'I don't need the bike!' he repeated. 'Because I've got Betsy!'

CHAPTER TWENTY-NINE

A Very Grand Entrance

'You can't ride Betsy!' Grace spluttered, as the donkey hee-hawed and tried to reverse into some bushes at the sight of the striding cyclops.

'Donkeys are strong,' said Mr Harris. 'Anyway, I'm not going to sit on her. Now, Shrimp Boy, go and fetch the roller-skates I spied outside the cave.'

When Frank returned with the sparkly silver roller-skates, Mr Harris stepped into them and immediately fell over.

'Jeepers,' said Grace. 'This is going to be fun.'

The cyclops hauled himself up using Betsy's tail, nearly pulling her over. Grabbing the reins,

he nodded at Grace to show he was ready to start the journey.

'She's going to pull you along?' asked Grace, looking worried. 'She's only small.'

'What are you trying to say, Doughnut Lady?' asked Mr Harris, rubbing his enormous belly.

'Nothing!' said Grace brightly. 'Ready?'

'Born ready,' muttered the cyclops, leaning forward as though he was about to start an extreme, thrill-seeking ride.

Betsy staggered forward. First she jerked this way and that, stopping and starting. Then she began to plod very, very slowly. Mr Harris glided, at a snail's pace, behind her.

'Woohoo!' he shouted. 'I feel so alive!'

Grace and Frank giggled and slowed down so Betsy could keep up with them.

They took the suspension bridge Mr Harris had mentioned back over the ravine. It was super-modern, with conveyor-belt walkways – like those you get at airports – moving in both directions under an arched glass roof. Adverts on bright LED screens flashed alongside them promoting all sorts of goods – toothpaste, designer bags, perfume, fast food at Burger Thing. Monsters bustled past them, some holding maps, some carrying briefcases. None gave them a second glance, despite the donkey and the cyclops on roller-skates.

That's Monster World for you, Grace thought.

'I think that actually might have been quicker than the zip wire,' said Mr Harris as they emerged safely on the other side. 'Who knew?'

'What a surprise,' said Grace, wishing they had known about it before they'd had to zip, unsecured, over the droppiest drop she had ever seen.

They passed Eye-Spy Wood and the Ankle Grabbers' territory (Bruce was nowhere to be seen) before they reached Brutal Bridge, which was much easier to cross without Dirk to contend with. Mr Harris only moaned nine times about being hungry. Betsy powered on like a donkey pro, although she did occasionally look as if she wanted to kick the roller-skating cyclops far, far away behind her.

All in all, for Monster World, it was a relatively uneventful journey.

Frank phoned Max ahead of their arrival, so when they reached the driveway to Monster World Prison, they saw him, Dr Darvill and Beyoncé waiting at the door for them.

'Oh!' blurted Mr Harris. 'Quick!' With a spurt of energy, he leapfrogged onto Betsy's back.

The donkey's legs bowed but she staggered onwards, a centimetre at a time.

'What are you doing? That poor donkey!' cried Grace.

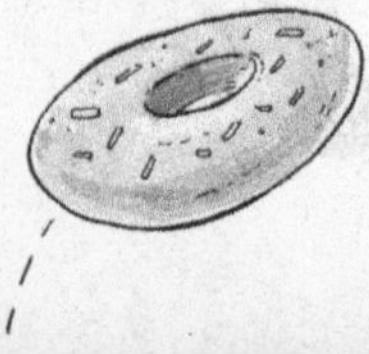

'Hush now, Doughnut Lady,' said Mr Harris out of the corner of his mouth, a fixed, smarmy smile plastered across his face. He was waving in a restrained manner, like a member

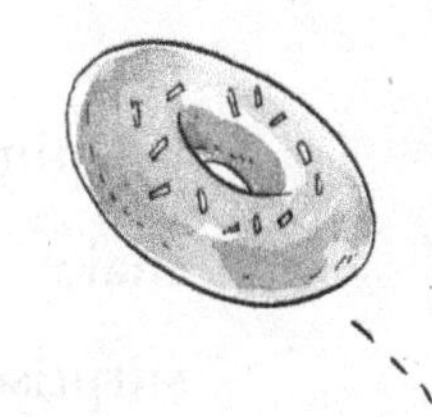

of the Royal Family, from the back of the drooping donkey. 'I'm making my entrance.'

Beyoncé jumped up and down on the spot, whispering something to Dr Darvill, who frowned and shook her head. Max was smiling, clearly relieved to see everyone in one piece.

'Senior Field Officer Mr Harris!' called Beyoncé, waving madly, as they drew up to the entrance.

'Miss McDonald,' the cyclops said charmingly, sliding off Betsy's back and forgetting he was wearing roller-skates. His legs continued to slide. Had it not been for Grace and Frank grabbing an elbow each and heaving with all their might, he'd have made his grand entrance by landing hard on his bottom. He kicked the roller-skates off in a brief tantrum and slipped on his old shoes, which Grace had taken out of her rucksack.

Max stepped forward and hugged Grace and Frank tightly, high-fiving Kenny with his pinkie finger. Then he extended his arm to shake Mr Harris's hand. The cyclops looked surprised.

'I'm glad you're okay,' said Max. 'All of you.'

The cyclops leaned in. 'Special Agent to Special Agent, I'm telling you now, Max Hunter – if I had even an ounce less muscle, I'd be dead. Thank goodness I'm in my prime.'

Max nodded. 'Quite.'

'Congratulations,' said Dr Darvill formally. 'It's been quite a day. I have to admit, at first I was reluctant to let you take on the mission of catching the escaped monsters, but you've done a good job. I was surprised to hear that Gerty Harris was involved – she has always been well thought of, a dedicated teacher. Mind you, it's always the nice ones who turn out to be as mad as a box of frogs, isn't it? I'm also sorry to hear that you were almost killed by an elderly cyclops relative.'

Mr Harris frowned, but before he could say anything Beyoncé barged towards him and gave him a big kiss on the cheek.

'He's b-blushing,' whispered Frank.

'It's the start of something beautiful,' said Grace, giggling. 'Or maybe just . . . something.'

'Senior Field Officer Mr Harris,' said Beyoncé excitedly. 'You are amazing! You are brave, fair, honourable and dashing. No wonder you have your own trusty steed.' She gestured to Betsy, who was lying, exhausted, on one side, her tongue in a bowl of water that a security troll had provided.

'Ah, you flatter me, Miss McDonald,' said Mr Harris. 'Carry on.'

'When we have debriefed here,' Beyoncé continued, 'I would like you to come with me to the Monster World Authorities building, where a panel of the most important monsters would like to speak with you and offer their thanks.'

Mr Harris raised his eyebrow. 'I'd be honoured.

Would you like to ride there with me on my trusty steed?'

Grace, Frank and Max yelled, 'No!' while Betsy let out a strangled bray from the ground.

CHAPTER THIRTY

It's Not the End

The debrief didn't take long. The recaptured prisoners had been quick to blame Gertrudetta for their escape. Some hoped that their sentences might not be extended. They had three group punishments imposed immediately by Dr Darvill – no board games for two weeks, extra chores including toilet-cleaning and rat-catching, and only one helping of jelly for dessert at teatime. They were all especially unhappy about the last one.

Grace, Kenny, Frank and Max agreed to wait in the prison guest lounge, which looked startlingly like a soft play area, while Mr Harris went with Beyoncé to the Monster World Authorities building.

By the time he returned an hour and a half later, Grace, Frank and Kenny were playing in the ball pit, while Max napped on a giant beanbag.

'There you are!' said Grace. 'You took ages! Did they spend an hour telling you how brilliant you are?'

'Yes,' said the cyclops, smiling self-indulgently.

'Bet you loved that,' she said. 'Well, we're ready to go. Frank found a Poo Shuffler in the foam shapes and there's something slimy right by my foot. Plus, I'm starving.'

'Me too,' said Frank, climbing out of the ball pit with Kenny on his forearm.

Mr Harris frowned. 'Doughnut Lady, can I have a word? In private.'

Grace scrunched her nose in confusion. 'Okay,' she agreed. 'But there's not much privacy here. Take your pick – the inflatable tunnel or the top of the death slide?'

'What a stupid question. Always the top of the death slide,' said Mr Harris, immediately marching off towards it. He was clearly feeling better. Grace dashed after him. They climbed up the bouncy ladder to the top and sat down.

'So, what's up?' asked Grace.

'They called me heroic,' said Mr Harris, grinning. 'And valiant. Said I have set an outstanding example to the Monster World community.'

'You brought me to the top of the death slide to tell me how brilliant you are?' asked Grace.

'Yes,' said the cyclops, nodding. 'But there's something else too.'

'Let me guess,' said Grace, smiling. 'You're fearless and brave and they're going to give you a medal for capturing all those prisoners single-handedly and escaping your evil grandfather for the second time? All of which you did with our help, in case you had forgotten.'

'You're right about the medal,' said the cyclops smugly. 'But there's still something else . . .'

'They gave you your own herd of donkeys?' Grace sniggered.

'A job,' said Mr Harris.

Grace looked up in surprise. 'But you have a job. With us.'

'It's part-time,' said Mr Harris. 'I can do other things too.'

'What job?' she asked.

The cyclops puffed his chest out. 'Prime Monster.' Then he clapped his huge hands in glee. 'Prime Monster, Doughnut Lady, of the whole of Monster World! That's how brave and legendary I am. There's never even been a Prime Monster before! They made the job up – for me!'

Grace swallowed the lump in her throat.

'Oh, wow. Congratulations, Mr Harris. That's amazing. And very important.'

He nodded eagerly.

'But it doesn't sound very part-time,' she added.

Mr Harris flapped a meaty hand. 'It's whatever I want it to be, Doughnut Lady. If the Prime Monster wants to be part-time, the Prime Monster can be. Do you know why?' He didn't wait for an answer. 'Because the Prime Monster MAKES the rules!'

'I see,' said Grace. 'Perhaps you need to speak to Colonel Hardy first and make sure it's okay to do both jobs.'

'All in good time!' chuckled Mr Harris. 'First, I need to go and check out my new office.'

'Now?' asked Grace. 'Aren't you coming back to the bakery for tea?'

The cyclops seemed flustered. 'Well, I was going to go now . . .'

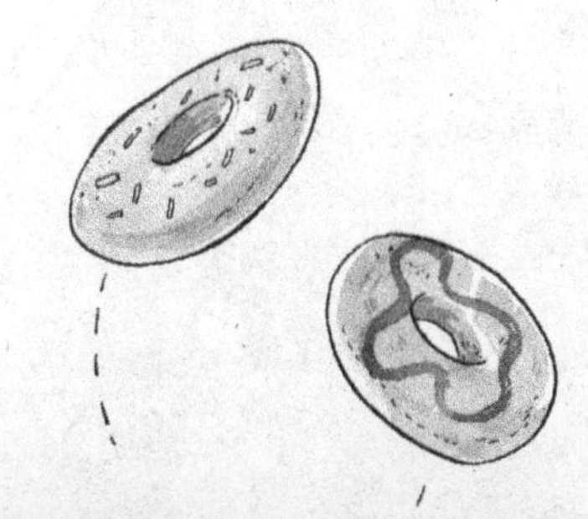

Grace couldn't stop herself. She leapt up and threw her arms round Mr Harris's neck. 'Please don't leave,' she said quietly, tears flowing freely down her cheeks. 'I know it's an amazing opportunity . . . I mean, Prime Monster! But we've only just started our adventure and . . . and I'd miss you. So much!'

Grace felt Mr Harris sigh and envelop her in a hug. He was surprisingly good at hugging.

'Don't cry, Doughnut Lady,' he said gently. 'There's no need. While I can't turn down the offer of Prime Monster, I will of course continue my work as Senior Field Officer, or perhaps Head of Fields, or Operations, or whatever. I'm certain that I will be promoted after this incredibly successful mission.'

'What about your room at the bakery?' she said.

'I will use it frequently,' he replied. 'I am shockingly talented at baking, and I want to continue using the facilities to perfect my techniques.'

'And you'll stay when you're working with us, and not working here?' Grace asked.

'Yes,' Mr Harris agreed. 'I suspect I'll need the odd break from Monster World. Signing autographs and having my picture taken will probably get tiresome eventually.'

Grace looked squarely at Mr Harris, her eyes glistening with tears. 'Promise me now that you will come back to the bakery for at least a couple of days a week. Cyclopes don't break promises, so this is important.'

Mr Harris gave a single nod then hooked his sausage-like pinkie finger round most of Grace's hand.

'I promise, Grace,' he said.

The use of her proper name prompted more

tears. Grace smiled weakly. 'Thank you. I know you think I'm bossy and annoying . . .'

He nodded vigorously.

'And you're grumpy, and you don't listen, and you constantly eat things you shouldn't,' she continued. 'But we make a good team, Mr Harris.'

He looked thoughtful. 'I probably bring more to the table.'

Grace laughed. 'Of course you do,' she said, standing up and wiping her cheek on her sleeve. 'Well, I'd better let you get back to the Monster World Authorities to see your posh new office.'

Mr Harris paused, then cleared his throat. 'Actually, Doughnut Lady, I'm a bit snacky. How about I come back to the bakery for a light supper first?'

The End

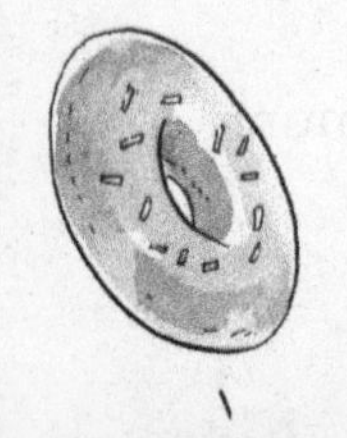

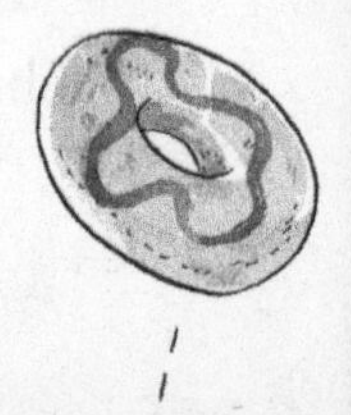

MONSTER GLOSSARY

Ankle Grabber

These are badly-behaved creatures which live just underneath the surface of grass, soil and mossy areas in Monster World. They are often mistaken for tree roots so it can be quite unsettling when they pop up, hand-shaped, and grab your ankles. They don't like letting go either. *The Monster Book of Monster World Records* reports that the longest a monster has been ankle-grabbed for is just over thirty-seven years and four months.

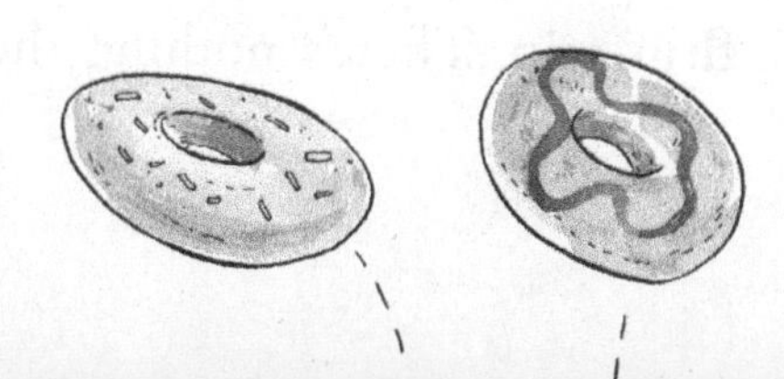

Biscuit Monster

These monsters are generally good-humoured and fun-loving . . . but they're tinkers for stealing your biscuits. Custard creams, chocolate chip cookies, bourbons, hobnobs, jammy dodgers, digestives – they don't care, they'll take the lot! They're often identifiable specifically as Biscuit Monsters because they are mostly covered in crumbs.

Bridge-dwelling Goblin

Like most goblins, these ones are unpleasant and mean. They lurk under bridges and enjoy scaring anyone who tries to cross over. Contrary to popular belief, they do not enjoy eating goats. They much prefer seafood and, on Sundays, a traditional roast dinner.

Cable Cutter

Cable Cutters have sharp, pointy teeth and a very firm grip. There's nothing they love more than chewing through the cable to a phone or laptop charger. These creatures are a little like batteries so this cable-munching activity charges them up nicely, while your sister screams the house down because her phone is dead and she's got four new notifications on Insta.

Cyclops

One-eyed and usually very large, cyclopes (sy-cloh-peez – weird, right?) made regular appearances in Greek and Roman mythology. Since then, they've evolved in a fascinating way. While most are still as thick as custard, some have gained intelligence. Most are self-important, some are power-crazed and many are happy to eat the problems they are presented with, especially if those problems are Gate-keeping trolls. Cyclopes love board games, bicycles and sweet treats.

Chatterbox Brownie

If you plan to have a conversation with a Chatterbox Brownie, be sure to block out a good couple of days in your diary. Although friendly and harmless, they can talk (without stopping) until you are scrabbling around in bins and other people's rucksacks to find something you can poke into your ears so you don't have to hear them any more. They rarely get tired and they rarely stop to eat. If, while you're with one, it decides to nibble a biscuit or have a sip of tea, take the opportunity to RUN! RUN WHILE YOU CAN AND SAVE YOUR POOR EARS!

Document Devil

If every office had just one of these, no important document would ever go missing. Gary from

Human Resources would never blame Brenda from Accounts for losing a holiday form ever again. They are the most organised creatures in Monster World and enjoy nothing more than collecting pieces of paper and filing them neatly and efficiently. They enjoy times tables, spellings and most puzzles, although they hate anagrams.

Freak-footed Troll

These trolls are quite different to most other breeds. They have the same self-importance and confidence but they have far bigger muscles and their toes are horrifying. At least one of them has a razor-sharp claw at the end of it, which is completely deadly. The others have gross, thick, gnarled nails which are often a bit yellow (pass me a bucket please, there's a chance I might be sick).

Fun Grinch

Have you heard of the Grinch that stole Christmas? Well, these grinches are very similar but they steal fun. Pop on a party hat and they'll whip it off before you can shout 'Hip, hip, hooray!'. Put up balloons and a banner and they'll confiscate them quicker than your teacher takes your chewing gum at school. Try to go the wrong way up a slide and they'll report you to the nearest Health and Safety Officer. You get the gist. Their idea of fun is alphabetising a thousand books in a library that's been trampled through by a herd of elephants.

Gelato Guzzler

These monsters are quite rare. Generally, they are found only in Italy or in specific parts of Monster World itself. They are flamboyant and kind, ready to make friends with almost anyone and anything. Show too much interest and you will hear their life story (their life-span is several hundred years, so don't say you weren't warned) while being force-fed the most delicious ice cream you've ever tasted. Their four arms make them excellent multi-taskers. Rumour has it that some live and work quite freely in many Italian cities, which explains the AMAZING gelato. Most Italian humans don't question the four arms, they just appreciate the ice cream they get to take to their nonna's every Sunday.

Giant Bat

It might seem a little patronising that I am explaining what a Giant Bat is when it's pretty blooming obvious. But, there might be a couple

of things you don't already know. For example, they are almost all exceedingly grumpy and bad tempered. They are often used as delivery creatures in Monster World, which isn't a great idea given their impatience when someone doesn't immediately open a door they've flapped their wings on. However, they do love uniforms, so wear their delivery outfits with aplomb.

Goblin

If you Google 'Goblin', you'll be told they are mythical creatures who are almost always small and mischievous (or outright malicious), and greedy, especially for gold and jewels. This is partially true. What Google doesn't tell you is that they come in many forms and breeds, including: Large-eared, Small-eared, Pointy-eared, Lesser-wrinkled and Sharp-toothed. They are generally stupid and unpleasant and will often resort to violence even when a sensible chat could sort out a tricky situation.

Gobstopper Grub

The only purpose of these round little monsters is to be eaten. They are a variety of wild colours and flavours. When they reach maturity, they voluntarily pop themselves into a shop display or a supermarket trolley, keenly waiting to be devoured by the nearest snacky creature.

Gossip Giver

You know when your grandad looks slyly at his friend, Albert, and says he has heard something interesting about Jeff from the golf club? That's probably because a Gossip Giver has spread a mischievous rumour. For example, they might have popped a bottle of hair growth shampoo in Jeff's golf bag when he really didn't need it, making people assume Jeff is concerned about going bald. It won't matter if Jeff has the thickest, most luxurious mop of hair in Great Britain, a Gossip Giver will love creating the gossip in the first place. The more people talk about it, the bigger and stronger a Gossip Giver gets. All of them have huge ears and mouths, and their beady eyes don't miss ANYTHING.

Homework Taker

The clue is in the name of these sneaky creatures. Their favourite thing in the world is that homework you painstakingly put in your school bag ready to hand in. They will swipe it and read it, and you'll most likely never see it again. Unless it's boring. Then they will put it back somewhere you have already looked for it.

Key Catcher

By far the most helpful and loyal species of monster, Key Catchers are affectionate, brave,

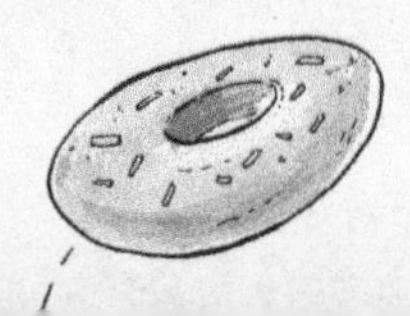

resilient and strong, despite their tiny size and wire-like build. They make excellent companions and are especially useful if you are the sort of person who forgets your keys and regularly locks themselves out of the house. Key Catchers can lock and unlock anything in seconds. They also have a mischievous streak and will sometime play tricks on humans, hanging on to a key from inside a lock. So, when your Uncle Brian is sprinting towards the cupboard that holds his fifteen-year-old can of WD40, just hold a cornflake cake by the sticky lock. Key Catchers love them so it'll be out in seconds, leaving Uncle Brian completely baffled at how you unlocked the door he quietly cursed at.

Large-eared Goblin

This is just one of the many types of goblin residing in Monster World. Like most goblins, they are generally unpleasant and fighty. It will come as no surprise that this particular breed has very large ears, which tend to be nobbly and gnarly, and have big tufts of hair growing out of them.

Leprechaun

Traditionally from Irish folklore, leprechauns are mischievous characters and tend to be associated with hiding pots of gold at the ends of rainbows. But, take it from me, they don't hide the gold, they help themselves to it. That's why we can never, ever find that big shiny pot when we look ourselves! They're generally not nasty creatures but they do have some questionable habits – nose picking, belching, drinking straight from a carton of milk, choosing a biscuit then putting it back with their bogey-covered fingers, only to pick up the one next to it – that sort of thing.

Lesser-known Human-faced Troll

This is a quick one to explain. They don't exist. Max made them up so he wasn't attacked by a cake-wanting queue of monsters who had escaped from prison. All of those monsters were so distracted by the mention of cake, they didn't notice for a minute that they were being ordered into a line by a man that clearly didn't look remotely like a troll. Phew.

Non-compliant Giant

A small number of these creatures can be very dangerous. Some like bone-crushing and people-squashing. However, many of them are much less harmful and simply don't enjoy keeping to the rules. They can be rather sulky and whiny, and some have a tendency to throw impressive tantrums, a bit like a toddler. Not a major issue in the grand scheme of things, apart from when you consider most are over ten feet tall. When a Non-compliant Giant throws its toys out of the pram, there's a very real chance you'll be knocked unconscious.

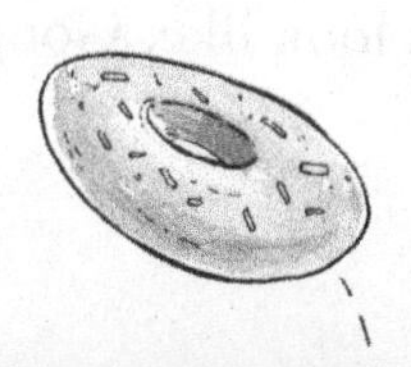

Parent Punisher

These are interesting and rebellious monsters. They don't take kindly to children being told off so when this sort of unpleasant scenario occurs, they will almost always do something to take revenge against the teller-offer. Whether it's a tiny poo in the coffee granules, or a quick wipe of a toothbrush round the toilet, these creatures are known for their loyalty to kids everywhere, and their wild creativity in punishments.

Pickpocket Pixie

If you don't know what an aye-aye monkey's fingers look like, Google it NOW!

Got a picture? Those freakishly long-fingered hands are an exact replica of a Pickpocket Pixie's, just slightly bigger. They flutter round soundlessly, poking their hands into pockets, shopping bags, rucksacks and purses. They will pilfer anything. They just like other people's things, whether it's a diamond ring, an old shopping list, a snotty tissue or a half-eaten Mars bar.

Pie Pincher

Pie Pinchers lurk around bakeries and the pastry section in supermarkets. There is no pie that this funny little beast won't pinch. Apple, cherry, pecan, chicken and ham, steak and ale, butternut squash and asparagus – anything with a pastry lid is at risk.

Poo Shuffler

Have you ever trodden in a dog poo you just didn't see? You probably only found out because you trod it into the carpet when you got home and your parents went nuts. Poo Shufflers do exactly what their name suggests. They shuffle poos into your path, watch the consequences and laugh. A lot.

Prank Cranker

These wily monsters don't just prank. They CRANK those PRANKS. For instance, they wouldn't just superglue a coin to the floor and watch people try to prise it off with their fingernails or anything handy-looking they found in their pockets. They'd superglue that coin down and then cover the top with superglue too. Then, those people would find their fingers glued to the coin, which was glued to the floor, giving them a bit of a predicament.

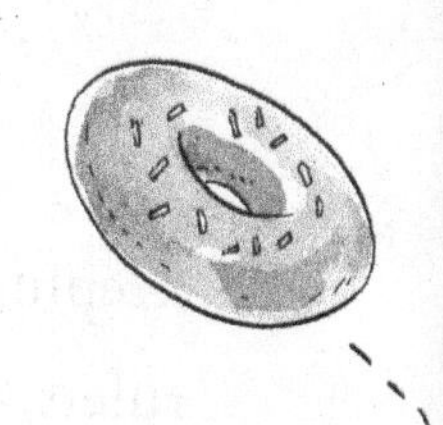

Road Wrecker

This one is simple. These critters wreck roads. Pot-holes, cracks, missing yellow lines, extra yellow lines, no lines whatsoever – all down to Road Wreckers.

Why do they do it? No idea. Legend says that the very first Road Wrecker had a falling out with the local council and started its road wrecking hobby to get on that same council's nerves. It worked. And, now, growing numbers of Road Wreckers are getting on literally everybody's nerves all of the time.

Rule-keeping Troll

There isn't a rule in existence that this breed of trolls would break. And if they have anything to do with it, you won't break one either. Rule-keeping Trolls have a passion for clipboards, rulers, folders with dividers and lists of boring things. They are not the life and soul of the party but, if you're planning party games at your next event, you might want to invite one along to make sure none of your guests get cheaty.

Security Troll

Now, if you know anything about trolls, you'll already know that many of them take jobs in the security industry. Why? Because they like to feel important, boss people around, make up rules and sometimes, if the mood takes them, wear bomber jackets with walkie talkies clipped to them. They are generally excellent at their jobs because they refuse to believe they could ever be wrong and, trust me, if your name isn't on the list, you're not going in. (Unless you're Mr Harris, and then you eat them to overcome their efficiency and quickly resolve the issue.)

Shadow Stalker

Ever had that funny feeling something's watching you pick your nose, or lurking in the shadows of your brother's stinky bedroom, or chasing you up the stairs – even though there's nothing there?

Well, mostly, there isn't, so get a grip!

But sometimes, in extreme cases, it's a Shadow Stalker. Don't worry, they can't hurt anyone and they can only exist where there are shadows, but they can make their presence felt, and that's enough for most of us to be turning every light on in the house immediately FOREVER.

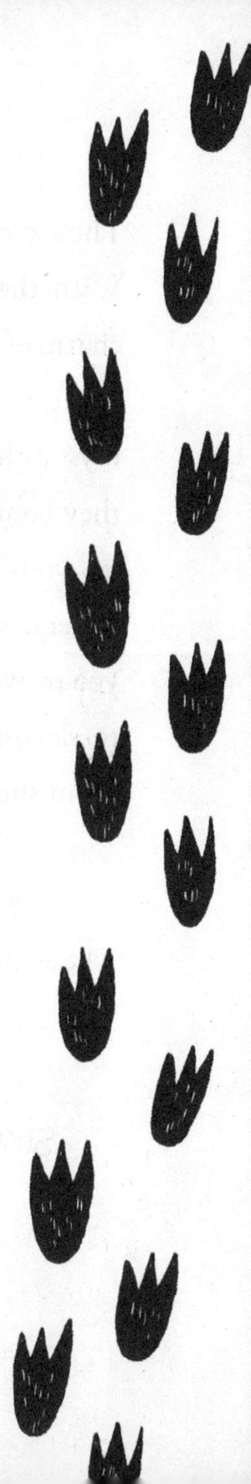

Sleep Stealer

These creatures do exactly as their name suggests. With their cuddly toy looks, they have all the charm of your favourite teddy and all the mischief of a gremlin. They will curl up in amongst your toys peacefully but, the minute you're asleep, they come to life. They jump on your bed, mess up your pillows, knock things over and cause general chaos until you wake up. Then, once you're awake, they doze off. They've been known to sleep for several days at a time. Almost all of them snore. Loudly.

Snack Snaffler

These large-handed creatures will eat anything.

Crisps, biscuits, sweets, they're not fussy (although they're not keen on rice cakes – too bland). If you're snacking on it, they will try and steal it. Or they'll lurk under your seat in the hope you'll drop something.

Sprinkle Sprayer

These are strange little beasts. Made entirely of glitter, they explode when they're exceptionally happy or feeling mischievous. They reform again fairly quickly, but not until your mum has spent forty-five minutes sweeping them off the floor, thinking the mess was almost certainly down to your little sister's annoying craft kit that she wishes she had never bought her for Christmas.

Tech Taker

These are relatively common, but mostly unseen, monsters. They can't resist a nice shiny electronic device and will steal any they can get within a couple of feet of. They don't steal them to play with though. Generally, they eat them. Tech Takers' diets consist mainly of mobile phones, dismantled laptops and tangy cheese tortilla chips.

Tickle Monster

Have you ever been tickled by your Great Aunt Deidre so much you've almost wet yourself? Well she's got nothing on a Tickle Monster. They have multiple arms and multiple fingers, all with super-refined tickling skills. They can get your neck, your armpits and your ribs all at once, leaving you wriggling like a worm and laughing hysterically.

Toilet Clogger

No prizes for guessing what these grotty monsters do. They thoroughly enjoy sitting at the bottom of toilets so their transparent jelly-like blubber spreads into every curve, nook and cranny. They'll block your loo quicker than you can yell, 'Fetch the plunger!'

Oh and don't bother actually fetching a plunger. No amount of plunging will get these bad boys out. The only way to do it is with a specialised blend of baking powder, yeast and icing sugar. In fact, I'd get yourself to Cake Hunters the second you find one of these gruesome grotbags.

Tree Hugger

Peaceful creatures, Tree Huggers live quietly in forests and wooded areas in small groups. They enjoy calm group activities, such as den-building and mini-beast watching, but, if the moon is full, they have been known to enjoy a raucous karaoke night.

Tripper Upper

You know when you trip over absolutely nothing, and your mum says you're clumsy? Well, it's probably not you being clumsy, it's more than likely a Tripper Upper being mischievous. These monsters camouflage into whichever floor they are lurking on and think it's hilarious when they pop up and trip you over.

Twitter Troll

In Human World, these creatures are unpleasant individuals who think it's fun to be nasty to others on social media, which is despicable. In Monster World, they are simply trolls who absolutely love using Twitter and other social media platforms. You'll have to trust me when I tell you that some of their Instagram posts are absolutely spectacular!

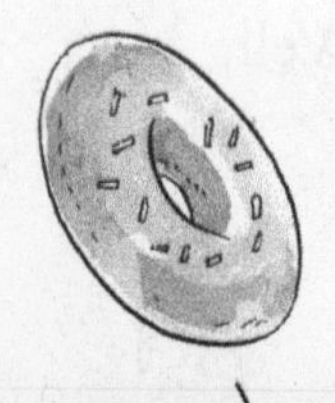
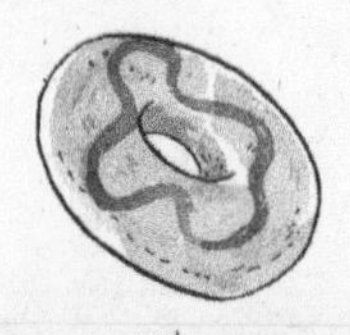
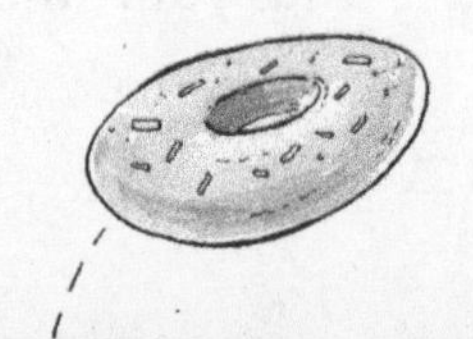

MONSTER PROFILE

Name: Gianna Pollero

Type: Author

Age: 44 years

Height: 5'2"

Weight: Not telling you.

Strengths: 4 detectable: kindness, sense of adventure, writing skills (hopefully) and sense of humour.

Weaknesses: 3 detectable: jelly sweets, cute animals, home décor shops.

Likes: Reading, writing, chocolate, animals, gardening, photography, arty things, coffee, Italy, interior design, architecture and fruit jellies.

Dislikes: Rudeness, artichokes, anyone unkind, being cold and wasps.

Best form of destruction: One tonne of jelly sweets. I will eat them and explode.

Notes: This monster likes to curl up with a cup of coffee and a book on a regular basis. When disturbed, she's very grumpy.

SCORING:

Friendship: 100

Size: 40

Courage: 62

Kindness: 93

Intelligence: 76

Loyalty: 90

Violence: 0

Danger: 5

Type: MEDIUM RARE

MONSTER PROFILE

Name: Sarah Horne

Type: Illustrator

Age: Unknown. Experts guess between 0-862 years old.

Height: 5' 6"

Weight: Somewhere between a flea and a sumo wrestler.

Strengths: Can draw pretty much anything, joy, compassion, fun.

Weaknesses: Stationery, Tuc biscuits or any manner of biscuit.

Likes: Drawing silly things, running up hills, Fruit and Nut chocolate, music and a good poo joke.

Dislikes: A lie, impatient drivers and seaweed.

Best form of destruction: Too much chit-chatting about nothing at all.

Notes: A Sarah is an elusive creature. In the wild she can be found painting large canvases. Sarahs are especially drawn to joy and whimsy, stories (especially the silly ones) and she loves creative, big-picture people.

SCORING:

Friendship: 100

Size: 55

Courage: 71

Kindness: 90

Intelligence: 72

Loyalty: 95

Violence: 0

Danger: 0.000000001

Acknowledgements

Quite how I am writing the acknowledgements for my third book I have no idea. If you had said to me a few years ago I would be doing this, I would have laughed and then probably cried because my dream of being a writer still seemed so far away.

I have loved every single minute of writing and editing the Monster Doughnuts books. My characters have become part of me and the writing process has become an integral part of my life. The more I do it, the more I love it. And I have learned so much on the journey so far.

There are always so many people to thank and, mostly, they are the same people you will see named in my other books. Quite simply, that's

because they're always there for me. And I will always be so very grateful for that.

Thank you to my brilliant children, Oscar and Sophia. They have no idea how much they help me but they really, really do. Sometimes, it's just because they're there and they're wonderful and that's all I need from them but, sometimes, it's because they talk through ideas with me, come up with amazing monster names and listen to the fourteenth version of a single chapter without moaning once.

Thank you also to my mum who reads everything I write within seconds and champions me and my books unwaveringly. She's always there for me, through thick and thin, and I genuinely don't know what I would do without her.

There's Maria, who this book is dedicated to, who keeps me sane and on the right track in almost everything I do. I was going to say

we've been best friends since birth but actually she's more than that, she's family and I love her with all my heart (as I do the whole clan – Amelie, Auntie Karen, Uncle John, Carly, James, Nancy and Nicola).

Then, there are all my other amazing friends who I am so unbelievably lucky to have – Helen, Lindsay, Tracey, Annmarie, Jo, Gemma, Aarti, Gillian, Clare, Hannah, Rachel, Richard, Ruth, Lynne, Julie, Liz (and all my other fabulous friends from VIAT), Claire, Paul, Amelia and Eddy. My lovely family in Italy too. And not forgetting my new bookshop friends who have been so very supportive of me – Cat, Alfie, Emma and Rachel to name but a few.

There are so many more people who have helped me in one way or another – I hope you know who you are and I hope you know how grateful I am.

A huge thank you to my ridiculously talented illustrator, Sarah Horne, who once again has managed to extract characters out of my imagination and draw them, nothing short of perfectly. Very few things compare to the joy of seeing the illustrations for the first time, particularly when a new monster comes to life.

Thank you, always, to Rachel Mann and Charlotte Colwill who give me their time and advice freely and support me unfailingly. You guys are the best – as is everyone at JULA – a literary agency I feel genuinely lucky to be part of every single day.

To Georgia Murray, my absolutely fabulous editor. What can I say? You make everything I do so much better – you just get it, and me – and for that I'm beyond thankful. And not forgetting all those at Piccadilly (and Bonnier) who have been behind me and my huge, bad-tempered but lovable cyclops right from the beginning. And thank you so much to Tia, too.

Lastly, I want to say an overwhelmingly huge thank you to all the lovely Monster Doughnuts fans. There's nothing I love more than hearing from you and knowing you have enjoyed my books. You have been, are, and will always be, part of something life-changing for me and no words will ever be enough.

Here's to many, many more years of writing and being lucky enough to call myself an author (*welling up a bit but also smiling a lot*).

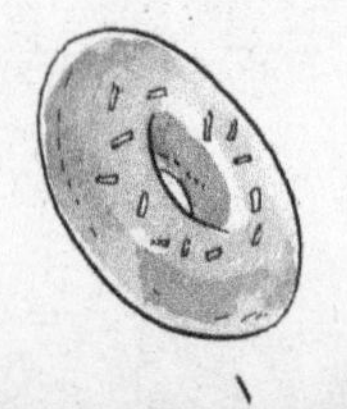
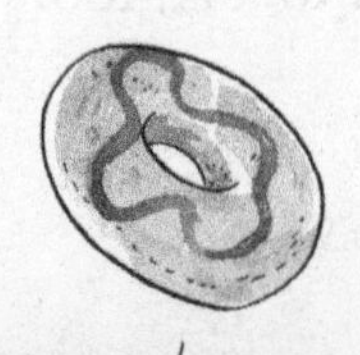

Have you read all the books in the Monster Doughnuts series?

'Delicious, dastardly and diabolically delightful'
JACK MEGGITT-PHILLIPS